Finding Ali

Stone Knight's MC
Book

Megan Fall

Finding Ali
Published by Megan Fall

This book is a work of fiction. Any similarities to real people,
places, or events are not intentional and are purely
the result of coincidence. The characters, places, and events
in this story are fictional.

Dedication

To my three beautiful children
M, S & C
Dreams do come true!

Contents

Chapter One
Ali

Ali lay on the cold cement floor, of the cell she had called home for the last six months. Her body and her head ached. She was utterly and completely shattered. During her imprisonment, she has only known beatings and starvation. All she knows, was that she was kept in shackles in the basement of a biker compound.

She had no idea who she was, or where she arrived from. The initial memory she had was of waking up in this place. Four huge bikers had surrounded her, and her wrists were tethered to the floor. The shackles were long, and provided her with some flexibility for movement, but the bikers converging on her didn't.

They had struck her so many times, her forehead felt like a spike had been pushed into it, and her face was wet where she could feel blood dripping down it.

She struggled to figure out how she had gotten there, but nothing came to her. She sought to figure out who would come to save her, but no face appeared to her. She tried to figure out where she came from, but came up blank. The only information she knew, was that her name was Ali. The head trauma must have been a lot worse than what she had thought.

Ali stared at the men that surrounded her. They were massive and intimidating. All of them wore leather vests, and their clothes were filthy and old. She could detect the hint of body odour from where she lay, knowing up close it would be worse. She was terrified and alone, certain no one would show up to save her.

She had screamed and wept as the president leaned down and tore her dress. The others had roared as he raped her. Then the kicking had started, and she lost consciousness. When she woke again, she was damaged so bad she couldn't move. That was both the beginning and the end for her. With her memory loss, she could only remember pain. She had no understanding of what her life was like before it.

The floor seemed colder than normal today, but that may have been because the t-shirt they let her wear had become thread bare and was starting to get several holes. She shoved herself into a sitting position and moved her shackles, so she could lean comfortably against the wall in the corner of her cell. The dim light made it difficult to see, but she recovered the mug of water she had salvaged from yesterday. Some days the bikers didn't appear at all, and she hoped maybe they were beginning to forget about her.

Just as she thought that, she heard the pounding of feet on the stairs heading down to her cell. She closed her eyes tight and folded herself into the smallest ball she could fit into as she recoiled in the corner. The footsteps halted, and keys jingled as her cell door was unlocked and shoved open. She held her breath as a biker came closer.

She had no idea how long she remained there as the silently biker stood over her. Confused, she opened her eyes and squinted up at him. He was older, and one she had never looked at before. His hair was just as greasy, and his clothes were just as filthy as the rest, but something about him seemed different. His eyes kept darting toward the open door, and he appeared almost nervous.

When he squatted down and captured her wrists, she cried out. Blood stained her arms, and her skin was raw from where the shackles had rubbed it, almost down to the bone in some spots. Tears pricked her eyes, but the man ignored her as he brought the keys up and thrust one in the lock. With confusion, she watched the shackles fall to the floor. Her arms felt light as the weight dragging them down was gone.

She was in utter shock, never having the shackles

removed before. The biker then thrust a pair of sweats and a new t-shirt at her. He angled his back to her and ordered "dress", in a gravely rumble. Barely taking the time to think, she wrenched off her t-shirt and replaced it with the fresh one. Moving carefully, she then put her legs in the sweats, and lifted her butt slightly off the floor to haul them up. As if sensing she was finished, the biker turned, and pulled a pair of flip flops out of his rear pocket. Dropping them on the floor beside her, he then headed back out the door.

She slipped them on then peered at the door he had left open. Panic hit then as she had no idea what to do. His annoyed bellow of "come on" reverberated through the open doorway. She carefully grasped the wall, needing it to haul herself to her feet. She wobbled a bit as her head throbbed and made her dizzy. She didn't recognize if it was the absence of food, or the head trauma that hurt so much. She supposed it was most likely a bit of both.

When she took a step cautiously, her leg gave way, and she slammed into the wall crying out. She caught herself from collapsing, and braced herself against the wall, as she struggled to take the pressure off her leg. During the six months she had been kept here, she guessed her right leg had been broken four times. With no medical aid, it had never completely healed. The broken bones had just fused themselves together, at whatever angle they had been left at. After a minute, she placed her leg back down and took a cautious step forward, willing it to support her. It did, but she was shaking, and it was extremely painful.

She heard a groan from the door, then the biker was beside her, hoisting her up, and carrying her up the stairs. She clung to him, frightened he was going to drop her. He kicked another door open, at the top of the stairs, and then they were outside. The bright light stung her eyes, but the heat of the sun warmed her chilled skin.

He quickly strode across the compound, and out a break, in the chain-link fence. No one was around, and she estimated it had to be pretty early in the morning. She chanced a quick glimpse in each direction and noticed he was headed down a small road towards a pretty beat up Honda. He adjusted his hold on her, so he could open the door, and then pretty much dumped her in the driver's seat. He slammed it closed behind her.

She stared agape at the man, as he shifted away from her, and headed back towards the break in the fence.

"Use the map on the seat, and head towards the address on the sticky note. Don't stop until you get there, because they'll be right behind you," he grunted before disappearing through the fence.

She peered at the map for a minute, then looked at the address. Her leg was throbbing, but she shoved the pain to the back of her mind and pushed down on the petal, as she started the car. A quick glance at the gas gage told her the tank was full, so she thrust the car in drive and tore away.

Chapter Two
Dragon

Dragon slammed the empty whiskey glass on top of the bar. Their prospect Trike, rushed over to refill it, snatching the whiskey on the way. He tipped the bottle, filling the glass, then shifted to head back to the other side of the bar. Dragon grabbed the back of his cut, reaching over the bar to yank the whiskey bottle out of Trike's fist. Trike nodded in apology, then strolled away.

It had been six months since Ali had died. Six months, since he had stood on the side of the road screaming, as her car was consumed by the flames. He was told a bomb had been planted in it and was set to go off about five minutes after she left the compound. He had given her a long wet kiss and told her he loved her, then watched her walk away.

She had gotten in her car, and he watched as Dagger had

waved her through the gate. Once the gate was sealed again, he had turned and headed back to the clubhouse. The explosion he heard had shaken the ground, and he twisted in time to witness the flames shoot into the sky just down the road.

He stood for a minute, unsure of what he was seeing. Then someone slammed into his back as bikers poured out of the compound and raced for the gate. Dagger already had the gates opening and had wedged himself through the narrow gap. By the time it was completely open the men had reached it, and they drew their guns as they raced down the road. That got him moving, and he rushed to the gates, passing several others in his haste. The scene that greeted him, would be forever burned into his head. Ali's car was engulfed in flames, as the bikers stared at in horror.

He continued running though, and it took six bikers to stop him from charging straight to the burning car. He struggled, punching and kicking at anything he could reach. Screams tore from his mouth as he struggled to get to the car. He was desperate to save his Ali. Eventually he was tackled to the ground, and he helplessly watched, as the car was destroyed.

When the flames died down, there wasn't much left of the car, or of him. There was positively no way Ali could have survived, and he could only hope that the bomb had killed her, and that she was dead before the flames had tore through the vehicle.

They had a funeral without a body. After that, he had picked up a bottle, and he hadn't set it down since. Club whores had sought to get his attention, but when he threw the third one out of the club, they had fearfully stayed away.

Six months later, they had no news on who had planted the bomb. No one had moved forward with anything, and no further incidents had occurred. The leads were all exhausted, along with his heart. Ali was his life, and with her gone, he wished nothing more than to follow her.

In desperation, the club had voted him in as the new Sargent of Arms. With no emotions left, it was the perfect role for him, and he thrived on the bloodshed. They removed his name patch of "Jaxon" and replaced it with "Dragon." He was a huge, terrifying beast now, and the name seemed fitting. Rumour had it he breathed fire, but it could have been the torch he preferred to use. He devoted his free time to lifting weights, and had bulked up, so it looked like he was twice the size he had been. His perpetual scowl helped too.

The bikers were a tight brotherhood, and they remained close to Dragon's side, making certain he remained out of his head, as much as possible. No one left him alone very long, and they all had his back. He was grateful for the brothers, and recognized he would have ended it long ago, if not for them.

He nevertheless thought about Ali. His dreams were full of her at night. She had embraced life, and she had loved him. Her parents were older when they had her and died when she was eighteen. She had no siblings. They met one day when he discovered her wandering along the road in the rain. He offered her a ride, and she had smiled up at him gratefully, and climbed on.

On their first-year anniversary, he gave her a necklace. It was a Celtic knot, on a leather cord. It represented soul mates. His father had given it to him and told him to present it to the girl who shared his soul. When he gave it to her, he had told her she was the missing piece of his soul. She had responded that he was hers.

One of his brothers had discovered the necklace on the road, beside the wreckage. He grasped it tight now as he had settled it back around his neck again.

Ali had been his girl for two-and-a-half years when she died. She had been twenty-two, and he was twenty-five. He could still envision her in his mind. She was a tiny thing, five two and maybe a hundred and ten pounds. She had long brown hair that tumbled to her mid back and the bluest eyes he had ever encountered. He called her Dewdrop, because her eyes reminded him of water, and because she was so small. He missed her desperately and pledged to never love another.

Dragon was drawn out of his thoughts as Navaho yelled, "unknown car approaching the gate, weapons out, let's go." He removed his gun from the holster at his hip and followed his brothers to the gate.

Chapter Three
Ali

Ali was exhausted, and her leg was killing her. She had travelled all day, and she was now driving into the setting sun. She was absolutely thrilled the sun was finally going down. Her eyes were used to the dim lights of the cell, and the brightness had made them tender. Also, she couldn't feel her leg anymore. The constant pressure from pushing down the gas petal, had made her cry in pain for the first couple hours, but recently she couldn't feel it at all. Her wrists ached and were still bleeding, and her numerous bruises and cuts were starting to make themselves known.

She was continually studying the map. Thank god, the old biker had drawn a red line along the route he wanted her to take. Without knowing where she was, and without a cell phone, she was essentially lost. She noticed right away, that the route was keeping her off the main highways, and consistently on back roads. She scarcely saw any other drivers, and she only passed through a couple small towns.

She had no idea where the map would lead her. The red line ended at a town called Haven, but the name meant nothing to her. She could be headed into further danger, for all she knew. She clutched the wheel fearfully as she continued down the road.

The old man had terrified her at first. She had never met him before and had no idea what to make of him. When he had removed her chains and disappeared, she hadn't known what to do. At first, she feared it had been a trap. She was just so afraid of the unknown. Having no others options, she had struggled to follow him. When he came back and carried her outside, she honestly assumed that her time had come. Having no idea why they had her, she guessed they were going to kill her then.

She had been stunned when he deposited her in the car and shut the door. His gruff last words had made her heart fly. Surprisingly, it also reminded her of a father figure. Without waiting for him to change his mind, she had taken off. It was heaven to be outside, and she didn't honestly care why he had helped her. Wherever she was headed, it had to be better than where she had been.

With her leg going numb, she was startled when the car started to slow. Apparently, her foot had slipped off the petal, and she hadn't even noticed it. With her eyes being so sore, and being so tired, she decided it was time to make a brief stop. She knew the biker told her not to stop, but she didn't have much of an alternative. She assumed she was a couple hours ahead of the bikers because she needed a small break.

Her decision made, she steered the car to the side of the road and headed for a tree. It was challenging to lift her leg back up and apply pressure on the brake, but she pushed through and eventually got the car in park. She had stopped, so she was directly under the tree. She found the release for the back of the seat and lowered it down a bit. It felt wonderful to relax for a minute and rest in the shade of the tree. She was still frightened that the bikers would come after her, and she was still nervous of where she was headed, but she took a minute to close her eyes.

Ali really wished she knew if someone was searching for her. She hoped she was missed. Not knowing had been gradually eating away at her. Were her parents looking for her. Did she have any brothers or sisters that were concerned about her? What about a boyfriend or husband? She didn't wear any jewellery, but then the bikers had probably taken everything she had with her, anyway. She didn't have a tan line on her ring finger, so she guessed she wasn't married. She loathed to think maybe she had no one. It made her too sad.

Her body was starting to shut down, and everything ached. Even her head was beginning to hurt again. She curled up as best she could in the driver's seat and tried to sleep. Minutes later she was out cold, both physically and mentally exhausted.

Chapter Four
Dragon

Dragon reached the gate just as it was sliding open. He stood beside his brothers, his gun drawn, and waited to see who was on the other side. He glanced over at his Prez, Preacher, who stood with his Vice President Steele beside him. Preacher nodded his head, the signal he wanted him on his other side. Dragon strode forward and took his position on his other side. Steele gave him a chin lift, and the gate grounded to a stop, fully open now.

As Preacher prowled towards the car, Dragon and Steele stayed with him. Not knowing who owned the car, or who was in it, put Dragon on edge. He liked things controlled, and he hated the unexpected. He moved slightly in front of Preacher as the brother moved forward. Preacher glared at him but let him stay just a bit ahead of him. As the Sargent at Arms, Dragon wanted to be sure he reached the car first. It was his job to protect the club and his brothers. If bullets flew, he wanted to make sure he was the only one hit.

Over the last six months, and since his rise in status, he had taken two bullets and had been stabbed once. The club wasn't usually violent, but sometimes things happened that couldn't be helped. The stabbing had occurred when he got in a bar fight, with someone that had disrespected the club. He had been drinking too much and had been sloppy. The gash in his side had taught him a lesson. He now drank but made sure he still had his senses.

The gunshot wounds both happened at the same time. Another club had surrounded a couple of their members at a rally, and a gun fight had ensued. Dragon took one to the flesh of his arm, and one grazed his leg. Both were minor injuries, and the club had jumped on their hogs, and taken off before the cops had arrived. He applied a bit of gauze once he got home, and he was good as new. Two small scars were all that were left.

Slowly, Dragon approached the car. Keeping his gun levelled on the driver as he tapped the window. The man behind the wheel was shaking and looked like he was about to pee himself. He looked to be in his late forties, and his hair was streaked with grey. Slowly the window began to roll down. Dragon leaned slightly in and took a quick look around.

The man had on dress pants, and a blue button-up shirt.

The back seat held what appeared to be a box of file folders, and beside him on the front seat was a medical bag. There were no weapons of any kind visible, and the man had both hands on the steering wheel.

"Get out of the car," Dragon growled. Then he took a step back, but kept his gun aimed at the man. The man was visibly nervous as he opened the door and stepped out. Dragon motioned for the man to move away from the car, and the man quickly complied. With a nod of his head to Dagger, he watched as his brother jumped in the car and drove it through the gates. Once it was parked by the clubhouse, Dagger jumped out and jogged back over to them. When he reached the man's side he gave him a quick pat down and declared, "he's good."

Satisfied, Dragon motioned for the man to follow Dagger. Dagger swaggered back to the clubhouse, and held the door, as all the brothers and the man filed inside. His brothers leaned against the walls and crossed their arms, while the man stood off to the side, visibly quaking.

Preacher stepped forward and gave the man his death stare. Instantly, the man held up his hands in a placating manner and began to speak.

"I don't know what's going on," he blabbered. "I got an anonymous phone call about an hour ago, telling me to come here to the Stone Knight's compound. The man on the other end told me, that within the next twenty-four hours, someone would show up here that would be needing my help. I'm a doctor at the county hospital, but I do a lot of free work on the side. He told me I had to stay here until this person showed up, and that you would let me help." He sucked in a big breath when he was done and sagged slightly.

"Who was the guy that called?" It was Steele that spoke this time.

"I don't know," the doctor stated. "I was just told the injuries would be serious, and I would be desperately needed."

Preacher nodded and motioned for the man to take a seat. The doctor dropped into the nearest chair.

"Well then, let's take a load off and have a couple beers while we see who shows up." With that Preacher headed for the bar. When his brothers didn't move fast enough, Preached bellowed.

"Fucking grab some beers boys, the fun hasn't started yet." Shaking his head, Dragon followed his prez and grabbed a beer. Everyone else finally followed suit, but the doctor just sat there. That was until his bag was unceremoniously dumped on the table in front of him, causing the doctor to almost fall off his chair. Trike just grinned as he walked away to get his own beer.

Chapter Five
Ali

Ali woke slowly. The sun had set completely now, and it was dark. With no street lights to light the way, she found it hard to see. Surprisingly, her eyes adjusted quickly, probably because she was so used to being in the dark. Ali carefully uncurled herself and tried to straighten out in the seat. Pain shot through her leg, and her arms were stiff. She was glad to see her wrists had stopped bleeding, but the blood had dried, in crusty clumps. She'd have to be careful not to knock them.

She started the car and flicked on the headlights. Her skin was chilled, but with less than a quarter tank of gas left, she worried about turning on the heat. She had been cold for so long, she just shrugged, and reached over to grab the map. After studying it for a few minutes, she figured she was almost there. She was pretty sure the last of her gas would allow her to make it. She ignored the seatbelt, figuring it would hurt her too much.

With a huge amount of pain, she moved her leg, so it was on the gas pedal. Her leg felt like it was on fire as she pressed on the gas. She really wished it was numb again. Slowly, she pulled the car off the soft shoulder and back onto the road.

She drove for another half hour down the road until she had to make a turn. Checking the map, she steered the car to the right, and continued on. Fields flew by her on both sides of the road, and the darkness seemed to go on forever. Millions of stars dotted the sky, and the moon was full. The sight took her breath away. She had almost forgotten how big the sky looked, and how gorgeous it could be with stars. The cell hadn't even had a window she could look out.

The drive calmed Ali, and she was actually starting to enjoy herself. Even with pain, the freedom was thrilling. She slowed a bit and decided she wanted her last bit of freedom to be stretched out just a wee bit longer.

All of a sudden, a bang sounded under her car, and then it started to swerve. It triggered a memory of another car with a similar noise. She remembered the car was a dark blue colour, and it had been slightly smaller than this one, but then the memory faded. She tried to bring it back, but the more she tried, the more her head hurt. Frustrated, she gave up.

Gripping the wheel tighter, she forced her car onto the

side of the road. Once she had it safely in park, she leaned over, and reached into the glove box. Opening it, she was disappointed to find it completely empty. No flashlight, no weapon and no food. She slammed it shut in agitation and wiggled around so she could look over the backseat. As with the glove box, the backseat was empty. Crying out in frustration, she threw open her door. Knowing it was going to hurt, she lifted her bad leg, and swung it so her legs touched the ground. Grabbing the sides of the door, she pulled herself up, keeping as much weight off her leg as she could.

Taking her time, she leaned against the car, and moved towards the back, practically dragging her leg behind her. Immediately, it was easy to see the back drivers side tire had blown. With no light and no tools, she knew she was stuck. She panicked for a minute, but she hadn't passed a car in hours. The country roads were safe enough, and she preferred to be on her own until daylight, anyway.

Stumbling slightly, she dragged herself back to the front seat, and leaned in to pull the keys from the ignition. Moving out of the way, she slammed the door and shuffled back, opening the back door as she passed. Practically falling into the back, she dragged her legs in and reached forward to shut the door. Then she leaned back and moved around until she was comfortable. Once Ali was satisfied, she closed her eyes and fell back to sleep. Morning could wait, she needed her rest, and she wasn't too excited about facing the next day.

Chapter Six
Dragon

Dragon glanced around at his brothers scattered
throughout the clubhouse. They were restless, and it had
been about nine hours since the good doctor had arrived.
Some were still drinking, but most had given up, not
wanting to be inebriated if something went down. They
needed to be able to ride. The doctor himself had fallen
asleep in the corner of one of the couches.

Dragon picked up his cell and checked the time, it was
eleven o'clock. This was ridiculous. On the word of
some nobody doctor, all the brothers had parked it in the
clubhouse and were twiddling their thumbs. What a
waste of fucking time. For all they knew, it could be a
hoax and nobody was coming.

Preacher dropped down onto the bar stool beside him.
Obviously, the lack of action was getting to him too. He

pulled out a pack of smokes and took his time lighting one. After taking a long drag, he let the smoke blow out over the bar.

"Thinking maybe we should send some guys out in different directions, see if they spot anything," he rumbled.

"Sure, beats the hell out of sitting here with our fingers up our asses," Dragon grumbled. Preacher took another drag of his cigarette, then stubbed it out in the ashtray beside him. As he went to stand, his cell rang.

Taking his sweet time, Preacher pulled his cell out of his back pocket, and glared at the screen. After a minute, he put it to his ear.

"Preacher," he growled. He listened for a minute, then frustratingly bellowed, "I know who you are." As he listened again, his lips pressed together, and his jaw got tight. Suddenly, he leaned back with a look of utter disbelief on his face and turned in Dragon's direction.

"Are you fucking kidding me," Preacher roared into the cell. His eyes remained locked on Dragon's the whole time. Unease crept into Dragon's stomach then, and he straightened, instantly on alert.

"Text me the map, and we'll work backwards from here." That was the last thing Preacher said before he slammed the phone on the bar, nearly cracking the screen. He lifted a hand and rubbed the back of his neck, a tell-tale sign of the anger he was trying to keep in check.

Steele, reading the prez's fury, came to stand beside him. Everyone else stood and crossed their arms over their chests, preparing for the worst. Even the doctor had awakened from his slumber on the couch and was sitting up and looking around curiously. The whole time, Preacher kept his eyes locked with Dragon's. Dragon had no idea why, but he gave the prez his full attention. Waiting for news on what the call meant.

"Got a situation," Preacher calmly stated. "I'm not gonna tell you who that was, but I will tell you that doc wasn't lying." He rubbed his neck again before continuing. "Apparently, someone is headed this way, and they're hurt. Now, according to my source, that person should have made it here a couple hours ago. As that isn't the case, we need to go and find them. I need half of you to ride with me, and the rest to stay here and keep an eye out. Dagger, grab a vehicle and bring it to the gates, I want you following us. Doc, stay here and get ready, we'll need you when we get back." He stared down every one of the brothers before his eyes returned to Dragon's. "Mount up," he roared, "and make sure you're armed."

Half of the brothers followed the prez out the door, and the other half took positions around the gate, and on the roof of the clubhouse. The bikers were covered on both fronts as they had no idea what they were riding into. Preacher mounted his Harley, his lips pressed tight together and a grim expression on his face. Whatever he wasn't telling them was pretty bad. Dragon just hoped the prez spilled it soon, he hated not knowing shit.

As the bikes started up, the roar was deafening, and the ground started to shake. As a close club, the brothers exited in perfect formation, and tore off down the road. It was late, and they were in the middle of nowhere, so both him and Steele pulled up beside Preacher, to flank him on each side. They took up the full road. Preacher gave them a chin lift, then shouted to be heard over the bikes. "Beat up Honda, keep your eyes open."

Dragon and Steele nodded their understanding and scanned the ditches on either side of the road. That uneasy feeling came back and Dragon gripped the handle bars a little tighter. Something big was about to fucking happen, and he wasn't sure if it was good or bad.

Chapter Seven
Ali

Ali woke to the sound of thunder. She sat bolt upright and groaned at the pain it caused. The car was vibrating. The thunder didn't stop, becoming one continuous roar. She leaned over the seat, so she could see out the front window. Bright lights hit her eyes and made them run as she tried to come to terms with what she was seeing.

Motorcycles. Lots of motorcycles, and they were headed right for her. That meant bikers, and bikers brought pain. Scrambling for the car door, she threw it open, so she was facing the field. She grabbed her bad leg and swung it around, so she could heave herself out the door. Her leg gave out immediately as it touched the road, and she fell hard on the ground. Tears burned a trail down her cheeks as she watched the bikers get closer. She looked down to see blood on her knee, but then ignored it.

She knew there was no way she could walk, so she dragged herself into the tall grass. Hiding was her only chance now. If it was the bikers she had gotten away from, then she figured it was death she faced. If it was bikers she didn't know, she only prayed they were kinder. Were all bikers the same? She had no idea.

She kept dragging herself deeper in the grass, keeping low to the ground, in hopes they wouldn't see her. The further from the car she got, the better. She prayed they ignored her car, and just kept on driving. The old biker had told her the biker that held her would come after her, but these bikers came from the opposite direction. That had to be a good sign.

She hunkered down to wait, but as they got closer, they slowed down. She put her fist in her mouth, to stop the scream that was building in her throat. As if an invisible rope held the bikes together, they all pulled over at the same time, and stopped their bikes. The thunder finally quieted, as kickstands hit the pavement, and the bikes were shut down.

Ali peered through the grass, her heart pounding a mile a minute. She bit her lip and tasted blood. Holding as still as possible, she hoped the bikers couldn't see her in the dark. Her sweats were black and the t-shirt was grey. She figured she blended in with the grass and dirt pretty good. Not to mention her dark hair, and the fact she herself had to be pretty dirty.

She watched as all the bikers dismounted and headed as a group for her car. When they got close, the three huge men in front, broke off from the rest and kept coming. They all seemed to be on alert. Several of the bikers that parked up front had left their headlights on, and they were aimed directly at her car so the men could see.

The largest of the three stopped the other two when they reached the car, by putting his first in the air. He scanned the road and fields around the car for a minute, before he turned to the driver's side, and opened the door. With the door open and the interior light coming on, Ali got a perfect view of him.

He was quite big. He had thick arms, and his muscles bulged, as he leaned across the seat to open the glove box. He wore a tight black t-shirt and his cut. Several black tattoos covered his arms. His hair was darker than hers and almost appeared black. It was shaggy and fell just past his shoulders, curling slightly around his ears. His face was scruffy as if he hadn't shaved in weeks. His mouth was firmly set in a scowl, and it gave him a scary and menacing quality.

As she started at him, she pictured another man's face. He had the same colour hair, but it was cut shorter, and parted to the side. His face was clean shaven, and he was smiling. He wore the same black shirt and cut, but he didn't have quite as many tattoos, and wasn't quite as big. Stunned, she blinked, and the image was suddenly gone.

Ali jumped when the man slammed the door and started to walk to the other side of the car, the side that was closer to her. The other two bikers stepped forward and joined him as he pointed out the grass that had been trampled down. Unknowingly, she had made a path where she had dragged herself through it.

She trembled, and held her breath, as the bikers followed the grass trail and stopped right in front of her. All she could do now was cower and wait to see what they would do with her.

Chapter Eight
Dragon

Dragon followed the trail of the matted down grass, with Preacher and Steele on either side. The back-passenger door had been left open, and it appeared someone had dragged themselves through the grass. The three of them only went about a dozen steps before they came across someone curled up at the end.

Dragon stared at the small form in front of him. The person was tiny and wore sweats and a t-shirt. The hair was dark, but being so stringy and dirty, he couldn't quite make out the colour. It was long though, and was a ratted mess, hanging over her body. From the size and hair, Dragon figured it was a young girl. The girls head was tucked into her legs, as she tried to turn herself into the smallest form possible, so he couldn't get a good look at her face. The girl wore no shoes, and her feet were absolutely black on the bottom. Small cuts and several dark bruises covered the girls arm.

"What the fucking hell?" It was Steele that voiced what all three of them were thinking. His fists were clenched, and his arms were crossed. He was staring at the girl furiously.

Dragon glared at him as the girl visibly trembled. Crouching down, he tried to get a better look. Something about the girl was familiar! Reaching out, he placed his hand on one of her bare feet. The girl screamed and jerked her foot away, trying to pull her sweatpants over it. Then he watched in astonishment, as she dragged her body away from him, and further into grass.

Steele lost his patience then, and took a step forward, growling.

"We aren't here to hurt you. For god's sake," he told the girl in exasperation. He took another step and then froze as the girl lifted her head to stare at them.

Time stopped, as Dragon got a look at the girl's face. It was covered in dirt, and the tears that ran from her eyes left muddy streaks down her cheeks. It looked like she had a black eye and a split lip, but it was hard to tell. Dried blood coated almost the entire left side of her face, starting at her hair line and ending below her shirt. He couldn't see her eyes, but he knew they were as blue as the sky. It was a face he would never forget, and even covered in dirt, he knew it was his Ali.

He went to reach out for her again, but the terror on her face stopped him cold. "Ali," he whispered brokenly.

Her head jerked towards him, and so quietly he almost didn't hear it, she asked "how do you know my name?"

Floored, he could only stare. What the hell was going on? He would know his Ali anywhere. Why the hell was she looking at him like he was the reaper, come to finish her off? His ass hit the ground, as he sat there, unsure of what to say. Maybe she couldn't see him very well in the dark. His hair was longer, and he had a bit of a beard, maybe that was all it was. He decided to ask anyway.

"You don't know me?" He questioned her in astonishment. She stared at him, through tear stained lashes, and shook her head no. "Nothing at all about me seems familiar to you," he questioned.

His heart was breaking. Six months ago, she died, and now she was curled up in the grass in front of him, obviously beaten, and with no memory of who he was. All he wanted was to hold her.

She glanced at his brothers, before turning back to him and whispering, "I'm not sure. I took a bad blow to the head a while ago, and I don't remember anything from before then."

Dragon was visibly furious. What the ever-loving hell had happened to her. He had stood there and watched her car burn to the ground. There was no way in hell she could have survived. Now six months later, his Ali was in front of him, and it looked like she had gone through a shit ton of abuse. His hands clenched into fists, as he imagined what he was going to do, when he found the bastards who had done this to her. He couldn't wait to get out his blowtorch.

A hand landed on his shoulder, and Preacher squeezed slightly in silent solidarity. Dragon's shoulders relaxed, as he realized the club had his back. Whatever happened, he wouldn't have to go through it alone.

Softening his expression, he asked again, "what do you mean by not really?" He remained quiet as Ali's brow furrowed and she tried to figure out how to answer.

Chapter Nine
Ali

Ali stared at the three huge bikers standing over her. She flashed back to the first time she woke in the cell, and the four other bikers were standing over her. When the closest man leaned down and touched her foot, the heat of his hand surprised her. She still recoiled from the touch, but there had been no pain from it. The warmth of his palm was almost comforting, and she wished she understood why.

When he asked if she remembered him, she got another flash of the man's face she had thought of before. She stared up at him in confusion. Was it the same man? With shorter hair and a clean-shaven face, it could be. The problem was, she didn't know if he was a friend or an enemy. Her head started to hurt again as she tried to bring back up the memory. She put her hand to it, hoping a bit of pressure would help, and shyly looked back up at him.

His eyes softened when he caught hers. "I keep seeing another man when I look at you," she admitted softly. "He has your features, but his hair is shorter, and his face is clean. I don't understand as I don't remember either you."

He bowed his head and appeared sad. "Six months ago, you left the compound, and your car blew up." He paused for a minute, and when he met her gaze again, his eyes were glassy and he looked devastated. "You died Dewdrop, I watched your car burn."

Ali stared at the man. The name he called her hit her hard. She remembered that name. She couldn't recall him saying it, but the name was familiar.

Suddenly, he reached into his cut. The move startled her, and she drew back in fear. "Easy Ali, I just was to show you something," he soothed. He slowed his actions and reached again into his cut. He pulled out a paper of some sort, and held it out to her, silently telling her to look at it.

She peered into the dark and attempted to make out

what it was. Shock had her holding her breath, as she stared at a picture of herself, with the man she kept seeing. She looked between the picture and the man and realized they must be the same person.

"Breathe for me Dewdrop," he pleaded. She let out the breath she didn't realize she was holding and stared into his eyes.

"Who are you?" She questioned.

He smiled softly. "Yours," he replied. "I'm yours Ali."

Her whole body went on alert. She didn't remember him. He seemed familiar, but she didn't know him. He reached out further and motioned for her to take the picture. Tentatively, she raised her arm and pressed her fingers against the picture, making sure not to touch him.

His roar had her drawing back. Suddenly, he grabbed her arm and held it closer to his face. Her wrist was a mess, and she knew that was what he was looking at. He ran his thumb back and forth across her arm as he looked at her with tortured eyes. "What happened to you," he whispered.

The tears came then, and she shook her head, pulling her arm from his hold.

"We have to move," one of the other bikers growled. "Company may be headed this way, and I don't want to be caught in the open." The biker crouched down in front of her nodded.

Raising his head in determination, he looked at her again. "My name is Jaxon. I know you don't remember me, but you're going to have to trust me for a bit. I swear on my life that I won't ever hurt you, and I can say the same for my brothers. We have to get you out of here, and you need medical attention. We have a doctor waiting at the clubhouse. It's only about a twenty-minute drive from here. Will you come with us," the biker asked.

He then held out his hand to her and waited. She studied him for a minute. He was familiar to her, and she looked really happy in the picture. Taking a chance, she put her hand in his. His smile was breath taking, and in that very moment she knew she was making the right decision.

Chapter Ten
Dragon

Dragon couldn't stop staring at his Ali as she sat curled up in the seat of the vehicle beside him. It was like his life started up again, the minute she took his hand. His heart was beating again after being dormant for so long. He couldn't explain how happy he was.

When she had taken his hand and looked up at him with tears streaming down her face, he had immediately scooped her off the ground and cradled her against his chest. Even though she was terrified and shaking, she still wrapped her tiny arms around his neck.

He had set out with long strides, for the vehicle Dagger had brought, and ignored all the brothers that gawked at him as he passed them. He knew they were just as confused as he was at the moment. Everyone knew her, and everyone had been at her funeral.

Dagger opened the passenger door for him, and he gently set her on the seat. Then he grabbed the seatbelt and reached across her to strap her in. She cried out and pushed the belt away. "Hurts," she whimpered.

Without a word, he retracted the belt and let it slide back into the holder. Then he shut the door and moved around the front of the vehicle where he was met by Preacher and Steele.

"Dagger's gonna ride your Harley back to the clubhouse," Preacher told him. "I also have Navaho getting rid of the car. I don't know if anyone knows what she's driving, but I don't want anything to trace back to her or us. We need her location kept secret."

Dragon gave a chin lift in acknowledgment, then moved to the driver's side of the cage.

Steele stopped him with a firm hand on his shoulder. "Can't say I know how you feel brother, but I'm telling you right now, we all got your back. That girl became our family too, the day she accepted you, and we look after our own. Fuckin hell seeing her like that, but we're gonna make it right. Brothers till the end." Steele gave him a half hug, a hard slap on the back and then turned and stalked away. Preacher nodded then stomped away after his VP.

As Dragon got into the vehicle, he heard Preacher bellow, "mount up." Then the rubble came, and the ground shook as the motorcycles started up. It took a minute to get everyone turned around, then they were headed back towards home. Bikes rode in front of him, bikes rode behind him, and bikes flanked him on both sides. Already, his brothers had his back, and he couldn't be prouder.

A quick glance at Ali again, showed his Dewdrop staring out the front windshield. He doubted she even realized the bikes were there. Her eyes were glazed, and she was looking straight ahead. He figured her head was pretty messed up, both physically and mentally.

He took a minute to study her as he drove. She appeared exhausted. She was covered in dirt and blood, which almost hid the bruises and cuts he could see on the skin that was exposed around her shirt. He was apprehensive about finding out what other injuries were hidden under her clothes. He didn't even want to think about sexual injuries, but he knew from her condition it was a probability.

His knuckles turned white as he gripped the steering wheel. Six months she had been out there on her own, suffering fucking god knows what, and he hadn't even been searching for her. What kind of man was he? He swore she would never suffer again, not even a harsh word. Her recovery was all that mattered. He vowed then and there to see her smile again one day.

As they reached the compound, Trike ran out and opened the gates. Slowly, his brothers made their way inside and backed up, parking against the side of the building.

When he glanced over at Ali, she was sitting straight up in her seat. Her eyes were wide open, and her skin was a pasty shade of white. Her whole body quaked, and it appeared as if she would collapse at any minute.

He reached over and grabbed her hand. Her tiny fingers wrapped around his like a lifeline. "I've got you Dewdrop," he promised. Her eyes darted to his, and then she nodded. That was all he needed right then.

Chapter Eleven
Ali

Ali was terrified. No matter how nice Jaxon seemed to be, or how comfortable she was with him, she was back in a biker compound. Memories swirled in her head, one after another, of the beatings she had received. Of the times when she was so hungry, she thought she would die. And then of the brutal rape by the president, the first night she was there.

She leaned back in the seat. Her breathing was coming fast, and she felt like she was going to pass out. She couldn't be here, she had to get away.

Suddenly a warm hand grabbed hers. She looked up to see Jaxon watching her intently. "Dewdrop, I've got you," he vowed. She looked down at their joined hands, then gave a small smile.

He didn't let go of her hand as he leaned over and opened his door. One of the other bikers headed for him, but Jaxon waved him off. Then he hit a button on the side of his seat, and pushed, so his seat went as far back as it could.

Turning back to face her, he gave her a reassuring smile. Carefully, he placed one arm behind her back, and the other one under her knees. After a quick jostle, she found herself on his lap. Then he twisted, and they were out of the car and standing before a huge building.

She didn't want to see the bikers right now, so she shoved her face in his neck. He pulled her closer to his body and tilted her up so was curled more into his warmth.

Memories hit her again, but this time it was of him carrying her the same way, but in the pouring rain. She could even hear his laughter as he ran. As fast as it came, it was gone again, but she was hopeful. She was starting to remember, and it was Jaxon she remembered!

She felt him step up, and then a door closed behind them. She knew she was in the clubhouse now. Men stopped talking, and the room become eerily silent, but Jaxon just walked straight through. After a minute, she heard another door open, and then she was gently lowered to a bed.

She felt the bed dip as Jaxon sat beside her and took her hand once more.

"Dewdrop," he called. She turned in his direction. "This man is a doctor, and he came here to help you. I need you to let him take a look at you."

She glanced over at the doctor. His hair was turning grey, and he wore dress slacks and a shirt. A medical bag was in his hand. He seemed friendly enough, but she was still a bit leery.

She nodded slightly, and the doctor came closer. Jaxon moved, so he was still sitting on the bed, but now he was up by her head and out of the way. Thankfully, he didn't let go of her hand.

The doctor smiled at her. "Ali, is it?" She nodded again.

"Okay sweetie, I just want to get a quick look at you. My major concern is your head. I've been told you are suffering amnesia. He placed his hand on her forehead and gently tried to push the hair back. The blood made it difficult, and he frowned. She went to move out of the way. She was embarrassed about the state she was in, surely, she smelt as bad as she looked.

The doctor only smiled again. "I think before we take a look, we need to get you cleaned up. I'm sorry my dear, but I need to get this blood off you so I can see what injuries you have. Would you be up for a quick bath?"

She looked over to Jaxon, and he nodded, so she nodded at the doctor.

"Can you tell me if there are any injuries, besides your head, that I should be made aware of?"

She thought for a minute. Her leg and wrists were the only things that were really bad. The other scrapes and bruises would heal, eventually.

Quietly she told him, "my wrists are a mess from the chains they kept me in." Her hand throbbed for a second as Jaxon tightened his hold. "I can't walk on my right leg. I think they broke it four times, and it just healed whatever way it was left broken in."

Jaxon got up and stormed over to the other side of the room. "I'll run the bath water," he growled, and then disappeared into the bathroom.

The doctor smiled sadly at her. "Don't worry about him sweetie. I can tell, from the short time I've been here, that man loves you. It's probably killing him to see you like this. He's the type of man that needs control, and right now he can't control this. He just doesn't know how to deal with that. He'll have to figure that part out on his own."

She agreed with the doctor, but she was still worried. She still didn't fully remember Jaxon, and he made her feel things she wasn't sure she was ready for.

Chapter Twelve
Dragon

Dragon paced the bathroom as the tub was filling. If he could get away with punching the wall he would have, but he knew it would scare his Ali. He was furious. Those mother fuckers would pay. He couldn't wait to become the Dragon people knew him by and bring out his blowtorch. Death would come, but it would be slow and painful.

The water was getting higher, so he leaned down to check it. It was warm enough that it would heat her up, but it wouldn't burn her. He knew it would still hurt any open wounds she had, but that couldn't be helped. He turned off the tap. Then he reached behind him to the cabinet under the sink and pulled out a new bar of soap. It wasn't perfumed, so it should be easier on her skin. He then pulled out three huge fluffy white towels. The last thing he added to the collection was some toothpaste and a new toothbrush.

Forcing his expression to soften, he moved back into the room. The doctor had left, and she was alone in the room. He crossed to the door and flicked the lock. When he turned back to her, he knew she was panicking a bit again.

"Dewdrop," he said soothingly. "I'm not going to hurt you, relax."

Then he moved across the room to her and scooped her up. Instantly her arms went around his neck. Stepping into the bathroom, he gently set her on the side of the tub.

"I'm going to turn my back so you can get undressed, but I'm not leaving the bathroom. I can't be away from you right now, and I hope you can understand that. I'm also staying in case you need me. Once you're undressed, I want you to wrap yourself up in one of those big towels. Okay?"

She nodded, so he slowly turned away. He could hear her moving around, and it took everything he had not to turn back around, when she whimpered.

Then he heard her softly spoken, "I'm ready."

He turned, and made sure he kept looking at her face, as he went over to her, and picked her up. As he started to lower her into the water, he told her, "I'm leaving the towel on. It will keep you covered for now and allow me to help you, without scaring you."

A small tear fell, and she whispered, "thank you."

As soon as the water hit her, she screamed and tried to use her arms to pull herself higher, and out of the tub. He just kept lowering her, and eventually she was all the way in. His shirt got wet in the process, but he didn't care. Tears were streaming down her face, and it just about broke his heart.

He grabbed a cloth and wet it, then gently wiped at her face. Eventually the dirt and blood started to come off, so he added a bit of soap. Her black eye stood out more now, and her split lip started to bleed a bit. He ignored that and looked at her forehead. There was a fairly decent sized scar from the top of her hairline all the way down to the edge of her eyebrow. It was jagged looking and red, but it was completely closed.

Looking away from it, he put his hand on the back of her neck and lowered her further into the tub so he could wet her hair. He made sure it was completely soaked, and then he grabbed a fresh bottle of shampoo. Carefully, he scrubbed away at it, and when he was sure it was clean, he rinsed the soap out. Then he repeated the process, adding more soap and washing it once more, until it shone. Next, he got the conditioner, and worked it through her hair. When he glanced at her face, he noticed her eyes were closed, and a small smile graced her lips. His girl liked this.

When he was finished with her hair, he helped her sit up a bit more. Once she was stable, he pulled the plug telling her, "need to change the water Dewdrop." It finished draining, and she watched as he filled it right back up again. He loved that she seemed relaxed, and not at all frightened of him. It calmed him too.

Chapter Thirteen
Ali

Ali stared at Jaxon as he refilled the tub. She had no idea what was going through his head, but he was being so careful with her. When he left, he had wrapped her in a towel, and put her in the tub like that, she had been so grateful. His thoughtfulness was touching. She really didn't want him to see her damaged body.

When the tub was full again, he picked up the cloth again, and added the soap. Then he picked up her good leg and began to wash it. He was extremely careful around the small cuts and bruising, and he didn't wash higher than her knee. When he moved to her other leg, his quick indrawn breath caused her head to whip up to look at him in confusion.

His whole body had gone stiff. She knew her leg was bad. Most of it was an ugly purple colour from the bruising. She was sure a couple of broken bones were pushing against the skin, but they hadn't gone through. She had some scratches as well, but it was her knee he was focused on.

She knew her knee cap was broken. It was swelled up to twice the size, and the knee cap itself was off to the side. When she looked back at him, she was shocked to see he was crying. It brought tears to her own eyes.

"I'm so sorry," he rasped. Then he leaned down, dragged her wet body up to meet his, and held on tight. She was stunned for a second, then she wrapped her arms around his chest and held on just as tight. She needed the closeness just as much as he did. After being alone for six months, she craved the attention and concern he was showing her.

Another memory hit. He was crying then as well and hugging her just as tight. She was at the hospital, and they were there to see someone. She pulled back with a start and stared at him.

"Someone was hurt," she said. "I remember being at a hospital with you, and you were crying."

His shock was evident and then came his smile. It lit up his face. "Dagger rolled his Harley," he told her. "The doctors didn't think he'd make it, but he did. Do you remember anything else," he asked.

"I remember you carrying me through the rain," she

admitted.

He laughed then. "You insisted on going for a picnic, even though the weatherman said it was going to rain. You made me sit in the park with you, even as the sky got darker. When the rain started, you refused to leave, so I picked you up and ran for my bike. It was a wet ride home, and one of my best memories."

She remembered then. "We went back to the clubhouse and spent the rest of the afternoon watching movies in your room." She stared at him. "How could I have forgotten you Jax?"

"It doesn't matter now, you remember me, and that's all I need." He was quiet, and he watched her intently.

Suddenly something else came to her, and she frantically grabbed at her neck. Panic hit hard as she couldn't find what she was looking for. She started to thrash as she tried to get out of the tub.

"Dewdrop, stop", he bellowed. "You'll hurt yourself." He grabbed her arms and tried to still her. With her still thrashing, he let go with one hand, and reached up to pull the necklace he had on over his head. As carefully as he could, he dropped it over her head, and she instantly stilled.

"I belong to you," he whispered. "Body, heart and soul."

Tears flowed down her face then. The necklace was

against her neck, and it was still warm from where it had been laying against his skin. "And I belong to you, body, heart and soul," she returned.

Then she threw herself at him, and he pulled her out of the tub, dragging her wet body onto his lap. She clung to him, and when she lifted her head to look at him, he lowered his and touched his lips to hers. It was a soft kiss, but to her it was home.

Chapter Fourteen
Dragon

Things moved quickly after that. It took a few minutes, for both Ali and him to get their emotions back under control. Once she had the Celtic soul mate necklace back around her neck, she seemed to calm down. Things were starting to come back to her, and he couldn't be happier. He would never be able to express how elated he was at having her back.

He finished washing her broken leg, which was extremely painful for her, and then he did her arms. With her wrists being so damaged, he decided to just pat them with the wet cloth. Regardless, they still bled a bit, and he could tell she was trying hard to hide her pain.

Once he was done that, he turned his back, and she opened the towel and finished the rest herself. When she had herself covered again, he pulled the plug and lifted her out. The towel was soaked, and water covered the bathroom floor, but he didn't care. He took a dry towel, and dried her hair as much as he could, then dried her arms. He left her for a minute so she could get rid of the wet towel and dry the rest of her body, and grabbed one of his t-shirts, pulling it over her head and watching as she shoved her arms out.

He then helped her into a pair of his boxers, then carried her out and sat her on his bed. The top drawer of his dresser was full of her things, so he grabbed her brush and sat behind her, to start on the tangles. It took about ten minutes to completely brush out her long hair.

When the doctor came back, he moved to sit behind her and she instantly leaned back against him, grabbing his hand and clinging tight. His kissed the top of Ali's head and pulled her closer.

The doc took one look at her wrists and leg and insisted he take her to the hospital. She needed surgery on her knee, and the broken bones in her leg would have to be re broken and set. Her wrists needed stitches, and he wanted an X-ray done on her head.

The doctor promised he could get her in as an abuse victim that way her name wouldn't be released. Preacher arranged for the Stone Knight's to escort them, and Dragon followed the doctor in a truck with Ali. Again, bikes surrounded them, and Ali looked terrified.

Preacher had been furious that he didn't get a chance to

question her, but the doctor told him her injuries were too serious to wait. That meant, they still didn't know who was coming after her. Dragon had tried again to question Preacher about who had called him after the doctor arrived, but he was tight lipped. That meant he knew more than he was letting on. He trusted Preacher and the club, but this was his girl, and he wanted to know everything that involved her.

About a half hour later, they pulled up to the hospital, and Doc whisked them inside. With Dragon carrying Ali, they bypassed the on-duty nurse and headed straight for the elevators. Dagger, Navaho and Trike had followed them in, so it was a tight fit.

Ali kept her head shoved in his neck. She wasn't quite comfortable with his brothers even though she was starting to remember them.

Once they were in a room, nurses came in and got Ali in a hospital gown. She was then hooked up to a drip. They explained the drip contained fluids, as she was dehydrated and malnourished, as well as a drug to put her to sleep.

She cried then, afraid that she would wake up chained back up in the cell. It broke Dragon's heart. He climbed on the bed and held her, telling her he would be there when she woke. As she was falling asleep, he slipped his skull ring on her thumb. When she drifted off, she had one hand around the necklace, and her fist wrapped tight around her thumb. The doc promised he wouldn't take them off her.

He followed her as she was taken for surgery, then he stood right outside the room and waited. His brothers silently stood beside him.

Chapter Fifteen
Ali

Ali slowly opened her eyes. She was lying in a hospital bed and was hooked up to an IV. Nothing hurt, which was a good sign. She glanced around the room and found Jax asleep in a chair beside her. He looked exhausted, and she instantly felt sympathy for him.

"Jax," she croaked. When he didn't move, she carefully lifted her hand, and laid it on his arm. Immediately, he jerked awake. When he looked down and saw her hand on his arm, he swung in his chair to face her.

"Hey Dewdrop, you're awake. How are you feeling?" His eyes only held concern, so she gave him a small smile.

"Fine," she admitted. "Although I think that's the drip." Her voice sounded hoarse, so she tried to clear her dry throat. He reached around, and grabbed a cup, filled it up from a pitcher of water and placed a straw in it.

He then leaned down and pushed the button to raise her bed a bit. He brought the cup close and held it to her lips. Ali took a tentative sip, and when it went down fine, she took a bigger one. It tasted so good!

"How bad off am I," she questioned Jax.

"Well, both your wrists got a lot of stitches, so once the pain medicine wears off they'll probably hurt. They'll heal, but you'll have some nasty scars. Your head is fine, and the doctor is pleased with how well you seem to be remembering things. He said you should regain all your memories shortly. He stitched a small cut on your side, but other than that it's mostly bumps and bruises, and they need to heal on their own." He stopped and looked at her with sympathy.

"Your leg is the worst. He had to re-break the two broken bones and set them so they would heal right. However, because they were broken for so long, your leg won't ever be one hundred percent. Also, your knee was broken, and he had to reset that, and repair it with wires. He put the whole leg in a cast, and it needs to stay on for at least four weeks. After that, you'll be switched to a brace. He told me, that because it was so damaged, you're going to end up with a limp. He also said you may not be able to use crutches because of your wrists. You won't be able to put any pressure on them until they heal fully."

If she was honest with herself, she actually wasn't sure if she would ever walk again. A small tear fell from her eye, and she quickly wiped it away. She was pretty upset about the scars she would have around her wrists, but there was nothing she could do about it. When she remained quiet, Jax spoke again.

"Of course, you're gonna stay at the compound, in my room with me. I can be at your beck and call to carry you wherever you need to go. I want you safe, and that's the safest place I know of. Plus, I want you close!" He finished and gave her a look, daring her to argue.

She gave him a small smile. "Sounds good," she replied. He seemed extremely relieved.

"I still have all your clothes and stuff boxed up in the back of my closet, although you've lost a lot of weight, so we'll have to see what fits you."

"Okay," she said. "When can I leave with you?"

He smiled at that. "Actually, Doc said you can leave in an hour or so. There are no immediate concerns. He gave me a prescription for pain meds and some penicillin, so you don't get any infections, and you're good to go."

Suddenly, something slammed into the door and she screamed. They could hear shouting in the hall, and then the door was thrown open. Jax jumped from his chair and pulled his gun, aiming it at the door. She was confused when in walked the old biker that had helped her escape. Then in ran Dagger and Navaho, immediately slamming into the back of the old biker, and throwing him to the ground.

"Please," the old biker pleaded. "I'm here to help you."

Chapter Sixteen
Dragon

Dragon still had his gun trained on the man Dagger and Navaho had pinned to the floor. How the hell did he get past them? As one, they hoisted the man to his feet, but kept a firm hold on him. The man had his eyes pinned on his Ali, but he wasn't struggling to get free.

Dragon turned to look at Ali. Her skin was pale, and it looked like she was trying to get out of bed. He put his gun away and moved back to her side.

"I'm right here Dewdrop, ain't nobody gonna get fucking near you with me around." He leaned over and kissed her head, then sat on the bed beside her.

"I'm not going to hurt her," the man growled. "She's my god damned niece. I'm the one that got her out of there for Christ sakes."

Just then the door was thrown open again, and Preacher strolled into the room. "Let him go brothers," he ordered.

Dagger and Navaho looked to Dragon, then to Preacher, and released their hold. The man shrugged his vest back into place and took a step towards the bed. Dragon instantly tensed and held up his hand.

"Far enough old man," he growled. He had no idea what the hell was going on, and he needed some answers fast. He could feel Ali shaking behind him, and he reached over to pull her close. She balled her little fists and held on to the front of his shirt.

She looked up at him and told him, "I've never seen him before he came that day and let me out. He's the one that put me in the car and gave me directions to you. I've never heard anything about an uncle."

"Names Joseph Meyers, but people call me Old Joe. I was your mothers younger brother. We're fifteen years apart. She was almost moved out when I was born. As you can see, I'm the black sheep of the family, and they didn't really agree with my life choices. I left home at sixteen and never spoke to any of them again." He signed then. "When I found out my sister was pregnant with you, I started to keep an eye out."

Dragon stared at the old man and tried to get a read on him. He honestly sounded sincere. He'd never met Ali's parents, as they died just before he met her, but he had seen a picture. Old Joe did look a bit like her mom.

The old man was staring at his Ali intently. "Girl, do you remember when that lost puppy showed up at your house when you were little?"

She leaned away a bit from Dragon and tried to sit a bit straighter. Old Joe had her full attention now.

"That was me. You were sick with the chicken pox, and I wanted to cheer you up. You remember when your class went on that big trip, and your parents couldn't afford to send you? Suddenly you got a cash refund from the mechanic who fixed your dads car. He said he mistakenly overpaid him. That was me! I also recall you going on a date, and the boy got a little frisky. If I think back, didn't he show up at school the next day with a broken arm?"

Dragon was pissed about that one, but his Ali's soft giggle behind him, had him turning to face her. "He's right," she said. "My dad never did know why the mechanic gave him the money back. I remember the boy too, he apologized to me the next day, then never spoke to me again. The puppy though, my parents just assumed a neighbour had left him for me."

Preacher spoke up then. "When we found your necklace at the side of the road, I figured you weren't dead. How the fuck could the car have been blown to bits, but the necklace was fine. I spent two months searching for you and calling in every favour I could. I was desperate, and that's when Old Joe got in touch with me. He could go places we couldn't, and he had a shit ton of friends. It made sense for us to work together."

Dragon let go of his Ali, and threw himself across the room, slamming his fist into the side of Preacher's face. Preacher's head rocked back, but he stood his ground.

"You knew all that time that Ali was alive, and you didn't fucking tell me," he roared.

Chapter Seventeen
Ali

Ali was in complete shock. The old biker was actually her uncle. For years, she thought she was all alone, and that wasn't the case. Not only that, but they had kept him away from her. It was obvious that he cared about her. Why else would he have been looking out for her all her life? Also, he was the one that saved her, and that meant more than anything.

She listened closely, when Preacher admitted to knowing she was alive all along and was actually working with her uncle to help find her. Now she knew for sure that she hadn't been just left there. She had thought no one was coming, and now she was learning she had several people searching for her. It made her heart swell.

She was completely shocked when Jax jumped from the bed and went after Preacher. The blow should have knocked Preacher down, but he stood strong, and scowled at Jax, as he wiped the blood from the corner of his mouth. Poor Jax just scowled back.

"That's one free hit," Preacher snarled, "but that's your only one. Try that again and regardless of the situation, there will be blowback." She watched as Jaxon nodded in understanding then turned away.

Suddenly he stopped and walked right up to Old Joe. "Words can't say how much I appreciate what you did. I don't take kindly to being left out, but you have my respect. Thanks brother." Then he turned and continued back to her side.

"What happens now," she questioned tentatively.

"Well," Preacher started. "Doc gave us your release papers, so we get you back to the compound, and on lockdown. It's been too long, and Old Joe just walked out with you, so I figure something should happen soon. It's too fucking quiet. Old Joe, I want you at the compound as well. Ali, we'll get you settled, and get some food and meds into you, then it's time for church. Old Joe should know who took you, so we'll get our answers from him. Brothers, let's give her some privacy to dress, and then we ride back together."

Without a backwards glance, he turned and left. Old Joe, Dagger and Navaho followed. Ali breathed a sigh of relief. She was starting to remember all the bikers, but they were still intimidating.

Jax turned to her then, holding a pair of his boxers and a shirt in this hand. "Let's get you changed Dewdrop."

First, he had her lean forward, so he could undo the ties on her hospital gown. Then, he slipped his shirt over her head and in a sneaky manoeuvre, somehow removed the hospital gown from under the shirt, without exposing her at all. Once her arms were through, and it was pulled down, he tossed back the covers and helped her get the boxers on over her leg cast.

Scooping her up, he cradled her in his arms, and strode out the door. His brothers silently followed, like the intimidating giants they were, as they made their way outside, and then headed home.

After arriving without incident, Jax picked her up again, and carried her into the clubhouse. All conversation stopped when they stepped through the doors. Instead of cowering like before, this time Ali took a minute to scan the bikers around the room.

They were all watching her with different facial expressions. Some seemed curious, some concerned, and others showed no emotion at all. She recognized almost all of them, now that her memory was coming back. When she smiled shyly at them, she wasn't prepared for the roar that went up, and the cheers that followed. She jumped in Jax's arms, then giggled.

Navaho came over then and smiled.. "Jax will get you

settled. I'll make the grub and bring it to you in few minutes Darlin." She beamed her thanks up at him.

Jax stomped past everyone else, seemingly pissed because Navaho got close, and headed back to his room. When he pushed the door open, a big fluffy pink comforter was now on the bed, with lots of pink throw pillows, and a huge teddy bear. Ali stared at the bed in confusion, then laughed when Jax muttered, "fucking bikers."

Chapter Eighteen
Dragon

After Dragon had gotten Ali settled, in his new pink bed, Navaho had come in with a plate of French toast. Ali had squealed and practically tore the plate out of his hand.

"When was the last time you ate darling," Navaho questioned. His quiet tone belayed the violence Dragon could see simmering below the surface. Even Dragon himself, had to keep it in check, making sure he didn't hold his Ali any tighter, as she was currently cuddled up to him on the bed.

"I'm not sure," she told them timidly. "They only fed me once every day or so, and I'm not sure how long it's been since Old Joe got me free."

"Well," Navaho said. "I'm in charge of your food from

now on, and I'm sure Dragon here will make sure you eat it all."

Ali looked up at him, "Dragon," she questioned.

Navaho quietly left and shut the door. Dragon appreciated the gesture. He took her plate and set it on the nightstand for a minute.

"When I thought you died, I went a little crazy. There was a rage in me that I just couldn't seem to let go of. I fucking hated being without you. I drank, I was somewhat disrespectful to the brothers, and I didn't sleep much. My heart just hurt all the time. You're my light, and without you I was just dark. Preacher decided that I should embrace the rage I had inside of me, so he promoted me to Sargent of Arms. They also made me change my road name to Dragon. They claimed I breathed fire now." Dragon made sure to leave out his new little blowtorch fetish.

When he looked down at his Ali, he was surprised to see her crying. He ached every time she cried. He pulled her close and held on, careful of her injuries.

"I'm so sorry Jax. I'm sorry I forgot you. I'm sorry I was afraid of you when you found me. The love I have for you is so strong, it terrifies me. Even with my head wound, I never should have forgotten you." She was full out sobbing now.

"Dewdrop," he admonished. "All of that was beyond

your control. Just know you are mine, and I own you. No will ever hurt you, and heaven help anyone that gets too close to you, brothers included. My heart beats just for you."

He pushed her away slightly and wiped the tears from her eyes. Then he kissed her softly. "Now, you need about fifteen pounds on those skinny bones of yours, so let's start with this French toast. Then you can take your pain meds and get some rest. I have to go to church for an hour or so, and I want you asleep before I leave."

He picked up the plate and proceeded to cut the meal into small pieces, so she wouldn't hurt her wrists. Then he passed it to her so she could eat. She only got about halfway through when she had to stop. Dragon scowled at her, but took the plate from her and placed it back on the nightstand.

He then proceeded to shake out two pain pills and a sleeping pill. He handed them to her, with the glass of juice Navaho had left for her. Once the pills were taken, he made sure she was tucked in and cosy. Then he kissed her on the head, and scooted in beside her, to hold her until she was sound asleep.

Sleep was slow in coming as she fought it. He didn't know if she didn't want him to leave, or if she was afraid of having nightmares. The sleeping pills would most likely stop the nightmares, and with a full stomach and a warm bed, she should sleep like the dead.

He slipped out of the door and found Steele and Trike on the other side.

"She good," Steele rumbled.

"As good as can be expected," Dragon sighed.

"Church now, Trike will stay here in case she wakes and needs anything." Steele turned and headed down the hall. Dragon left the door open a crack, so Trike could hear her from the hall, and then followed Steele. He was on edge, and ready to bang heads. He needed answers, and he was going to get them.

Chapter Nineteen
Dragon

When Dragon entered church with Steele, everyone was already inside. He took his seat to the left of Preacher while Steele closed the doors and sat to Preacher's right.

Preacher started right away. "Brothers, you know Dragon's woman was presumed dead after the car bombing six months ago. As you've all seen, she's alive, and was being held by another biker club. Right now, we will fucking find out who took her, and then we'll reign hell down on those motherfuckers," he bellowed.

All the brothers roared their agreement and pounded their fists on the table. After a minute, Preacher held up his hands. The room went silent. He looked to the back of the room where Ali's uncle stood and motioned him forward. Once he was near the head of the table, Preacher continued talking.

"Brothers, meet Old Joe, Ali's uncle. Now when Ali died, I didn't believe it, and neither did Old Joe. We worked together, and Joe eventually found her and got her out. Now he's here to tell us all he knows about the bastards." He motioned for Old Joe to carry on.

Old Joe stepped forward and raised his head. "About a year ago, The Outlaws came to you and asked to start a club on the edge of your territory. You said no, and they went away. They didn't plan to ask you again. They took my niece to torture, and they meant to return her to you with a bullet in her head. They wanted you to suffer. They've already acquired more territory, so they don't care about that. I can show you where their compound is, but with Ali gone, they probably won't be there anymore. My guess, they're on their way here."

Preacher stood up again. "I want men posted at different spots along the road, in both directions. I want men on the roof, and men along the gate. If they show, we see them coming, and we fuck them up. Dragon, you get the blowtorch ready, it's time to fuck some bikers up," he roared.

Cheers went up around the room. "Meeting adjourned, brothers, see Steele for your assignments. Keep your weapons on you, loaded and ready at all times, and keep your alcohol consumption to a minimum. I need everyone ready for war." Nods went around the room, and the doors were opened so the brothers could file out.

"Hold up," Dragon yelled. Everyone stopped and looked back at him. "Old Joe, I need to know exactly what those motherfuckers did to my girl."

Preacher turned to face him. "Dragon my brother, this conversation isn't for the club. Old Joe, Steele, Dagger and Navaho, sit your ass down. The rest, keep on walking. Steele will be out shortly, so stay close, and close the fucking door after you leave."

When everyone had left, and the doors were locked, all eyes turned to Old Joe. He sat on a chair close to Dragon and hung his head. His face was etched in pain.

"I arrived two days before I found out she was there. One of them got chatty after he had a couple shots of whiskey. They got her out of the car before it exploded that's when she received the blow to the head. They used a piece of pipe."

"She woke up in a cell in a basement, and she was chained to the floor. She was beaten almost daily and starved. She had a bucket to piss in, and a bucket of water to clean with." Joe wouldn't meet anyone's eyes. "The first night she was there, the president raped her. It was only one time, but he had three of his officer's watch." Joe looked up at Dragon then, and he had tears in his eyes. He looked absolutely gutted.

Dragon was broken. He stood up, walked to the wall, and drove his fist right through it. Then he pulled it out, let out a roar, and did it again. He meant to keep on doing it, but Preacher was there pulling him back.

"Brother, go to your woman," he ordered sternly. "You need to be with her."

Dragon was halfway out the door when, Ali starting screaming.

Chapter Twenty
Ali

Ali was caught in a nightmare. She was back in the cell. The four bikers were standing over her and laughing. Then the cruellest looking of the four started to lean down towards her. She tried to move, but the chains held her in place, and she couldn't get away. She could smell him, alcohol, cigarettes and sweat, and it made her gag. She thrashed and kicked, screaming until she was hoarse.

Arms surrounded her, and a warm, hard body pressed her down so she was pinned to the floor. Terrified, she started to tremble and thrash. Then he spoke, whispering into her ear.

"Dewdrop, I've got you. You are absolutely safe here with me. Come back to me pretty girl," he pleaded.

Slowly, Ali opened her eyes. Jaxon was right there, and he had wrapped his huge, muscled body around hers. A couple tears fell from his eyes. She looked to the door, and there were several bikers standing against the wall. They all looked menacing, but they tried to smile at her, as they gave her pitying looks at the same time. Then in tandem, the bikers left the room, and the door closed behind them. Ali closed her eyes and broke into tears.

Sobs shook her broken body. Jaxon eased his hold and moved over to lay beside her. Then her tiny body was dragged across his as he tucked her head protectively into his shoulder. He didn't say a word, just held her and let her cry.

It took a long time for the shaking to slow, and the tears to run dry. Jaxon slowly began to stroke her back, and the shaking stopped altogether.

"You were raped," he stated.

She lifted her head so she could see him. Anguish was written in every line. "I'm okay Jax," she tried to soothe him.

He shook his head. "You're not," he growled. "But you will be! I'm gonna make sure of that," he promised.

Ali smiled sadly at him. "I know," she said.

He checked her leg and made sure she wasn't in pain, then he pulled the ridiculous pink comforter over them.

"Sleep baby," he told her. "I'll be in your dreams with you."

Ali closed her eyes and fell back asleep. Every time the bikers tried to get close, Jaxon was there chasing them away, just like he promised.

When she woke again several hours later, Jaxon was still there, holding her close, but fast asleep. She figured he must be exhausted. He hadn't slept at all since he found her.

She studied him while she could. She could still see the man he had been, underneath the rougher look. His hair was definitely a lot longer, but she liked it. The short beard was a big change, but she wasn't sure how she felt about that. She really liked it, but it hid most of his face, and she didn't like that.

She lifted her hand and gently stoked it. The beard was softer than it looked, and thick.

"What are doing?"

Ali jumped and her eyes flew to his. He was wide awake and staring at her. All the anguish seemed to be gone and amusement was left in its wake.

Carefully she shifted up a bit, then leaned in and put her lips to his. The kiss was soft at first, but then his hand reached under her hair, and slid across the back of her neck. He put pressure there, forcing her closer and his tongue nipped at her lip. She opened her mouth slightly and his tongue pushed in, accepting the silent invitation.

She was consumed by him. He completely took over, and his passion spurned on hers. She could taste his minty breath and his earthy smell overwhelmed her. She ached for him.

Then he pulled away. "That's gonna lead to things you aren't ready for yet. When we make love again, it won't be after a nightmare. I want you to be completely focused on me and the things I'm doing to you. I want you to ache for me."

She shivered slightly from his words, and from the smouldering look he gave her.

A knock on the door interrupted their moment, and she turned away.

"Fucking bikers," he mumbled again, and she giggled.

Chapter Twenty-One
Dragon

The next week went by pretty quietly. The club kept sentries posted, but there was still no sign of The Outlaws. They even sent a small group to the compound Old Joe told them about, but they came up empty. It was deserted, and it was fucking frustrating. Dragon needed to know where they were, and he needed vengeance.

His Ali was doing better though. Her lip had healed, and her black eye was almost gone. A lot of her bruising and scrapes had healed too. Dragon cleaned her wrists every day and changed the bandages. She cried every time he did this. They were healing, but the scars were going to be thick.

Finally he was able to take her bandages off for good. Like every other day, she cried when she looked at her wrists. He reached behind him and brought out two pink Harley bandanas'. Carefully, he wrapped each wrist in one of the bandanas. When he was done, he declared her his official biker woman. Her smile lit the room, and she threw herself at him. Dragon felt like the greatest man on earth. She'd worn them every day after that.

Finally, she was able to use crutches. This was both a blessing and a curse for Dragon. She seemed to like the independence they gave her, but he knew she loved being in his arms. Every time he picked her up, she cuddled close and shoved her face in his neck. Dragon also keep catching her sniffing him and sighing. He hadn't told her yet, but he liked to smell her too. He also kept conveniently losing the crutches.

Ali was also getting better at being around his brothers. She remembered them all now, and they treated her like family. They love her, and they decided to give her the nickname Tink, because she's so fucking tiny. All the brothers go out of their way to make she's always at ease. She's closer to them now, then she was before.

Dragon spent one day pulling her boxes out of the back of his closet. He found some long skirts in them and decided she should wear them instead of his boxers. Dragon missed the boxers, but she didn't like wearing them when she left the room. He could understand that as he didn't like the brothers looking at her in them.

Navaho kept his word and has made most of her meals. Dragon was thrilled that already she has put on a couple more pounds. Steele also surprised her, by dragging in a hairdresser he had slept with. The girl trimmed up Ali's hair and gave her bangs. Now the huge ass scar on her forehead is hidden. Ali cried when the girl was finished, she was incredibly happy. She even made sure to let him know how appreciative she was.

His Ali still has trouble sleeping and wakes up a lot now with nightmares. He started pulling her on top of him, then he'd place her tiny hand on his heart, so she could feel his heart beat. That seems to calm her down as she always tried to match her heartbeat to his.

Dragon came in a couple nights ago, to go to bed, and found Trike getting down off the bed. He had a stapler in his hand and looked guilty. Dragon headed towards him ready to pound the little fucker, but Ali stopped him. Trike quickly ran to the door, shutting it and turning off the lights.

The prospect had covered the ceiling in plastic stars. When Ali looked at him, he sheepishly told her that he knew she had trouble sleeping and wanted to do something to help. He wanted her to see the stars and remember she was safe. The ass made her cry again, and she leaned over and kissed his cheek. Dragon went to go after him, but he flew out the door before he could catch him, and that fucker was fast.

Dragon now had pink bedding and stars on the ceiling, his street cred was taking a big hit. To fix it, he brought in a big Harley Davidson rug, and stuck it on the floor by the bed. When Ali saw it, she laughed, but he just smirked at her. Things were definitely getting better.

Chapter Twenty-Two
Ali

Ali relaxed in bed. She had just woken up from a nap. She still found that she got tired easily, but each day she found it got a bit better. Today was Sunday and most of the guys were just hanging around and taking it easy. Ali loved being here now. The bikers treated her well and things were easy.

Suddenly, a loud boom sounded, shaking her bed. Men began shouting and boots pounded down the hall towards the common room. Then she heard gunfire. She was absolutely terrified. She had no idea what she should do.

Without warning, the door flew open and Trike stood there. The prospect was armed, and he looked furious.

"The Outlaws just blew the gates. Their men are

swarming the compound. I saw Dragon, but he's stuck trying to keep them from entering the building. I decided to come check on you. We need to get you out of the bed, and I'm thinking the best idea is to lock you in the bathroom." He hurriedly told her.

He moved quickly then, picking her up and moving towards the bathroom. Gently, he laid her down in the tub. Then he handed her his gun.

"I'm just going to lock the bedroom door," he said as he hurried out. She heard the lock click and then he was back. He shut and locked the bathroom door as well, with him inside with her. He then hunkered down between the counter and the toilet with another gun he pulled out of the back of his pants. He was a big guy, and he looked ridiculous, wedged into the tiny spot.

Ali was shaking she was so scared. She really wanted Jaxon and prayed he was okay. She hoped all the bikers were okay. When she looked over at Trike, she had tears in her eyes. She was so grateful he had stayed with her. He was risking his life to protect her.

He reached over and took her hand, and she instantly wrapped her fingers around his and held on tight. "It's gonna be okay," he told her, but he didn't look so sure. As a prospect, he hadn't been with the club long, and this was probably his first gun fight.

Men were still yelling and shots were still being fired. Ali sunk down lower in the tub and turned, so she was facing the door. She used her free hand to lift the gun, resting it on the side of the bathtub and pointing it towards the door.

What seemed like hours later, but in actuality was probably only a few minutes, she heard footsteps stop in front of the bedroom door. The handle was tried, and Ali fearfully held her breath. Then a kick was heard, and wood splintered as the door fell away.

Trike let go of her hand to get better leverage on his gun, so Ali put both hands on her gun as well. She was crying harder now, and she tried to keep quiet. Almost immediately the bathroom door fell to the side as someone broke that door too. Trike fired and Ali did too as the man that came into the bathroom fired his gun at the same time.

The noise was deafening, and then there was silence. The biker that had come in had two holes in his chest and he crashed to the floor. Ali was pretty sure he was dead. When she looked over at Trike, she was horrified to see his shoulder was bleeding and he was leaning heavily on the toilet.

She cried out and tried to scramble out of the tub. Her leg slowed her down, and it was really awkward, but she finally fell on the floor beside the dead man. She instantly moved away, not wanting to be too close to the body. She dragged herself in front of Trike and looked at him. There was a lot blood on his shirt.

Wiping the tears from her eyes, she snagged a towel and pressed it to the wound. Trike cried out and slumped over unconscious. Then she heard a noise and turned to see another biker standing in the door. She recognized him right away as one of the four higher ranking bikers. He had loved beating her, and he was the one that kept breaking her leg.

Trike's gun was laying on the floor where he dropped it when he was shot, and she had both her hands on the towel. The biker in the doorway laughed as he took a step towards her.

Chapter Twenty-Three
Dragon

Dragon was sitting at the bar with a whisky in his hand. His Ali was napping, and he knew she wouldn't sleep with him in the room. She told him he was a distraction. He loved that she felt that way.

He was about to take a sip when Steele's phone went off, immediately followed by Preacher's and his. They all looked at each other and the room went silent as his brothers looked their way too.

Preacher answered his and then bellowed. "Outlaws riding in hard, pieces out now and move."

Then before the brothers could blink, a loud boom sounded near the front of the clubhouse. Everyone jumped up and bolted for the front door. Once outside, they found the front gate laying on the ground. Motorcycles were pouring in and bullets starting flying.

Dragon took cover behind a cage and started firing. All the brothers were outside now and were firing too. Bullets were flying, men were shouting, and bodies were falling. Thankfully, it looked like only the Outlaws were falling. Some brothers he could see were bleeding, but they were all standing.

He saw five Outlaws making their way to the doors of the clubhouse. He took a quick look around and saw the dumpster close to the door. He ran. A bullet hit the ground in front of him, he turned and fired. A grunt followed, but he didn't bother looking. When he hit the dumpster, he fired two shots at the men running for the door. His shots were deadly, two men fell, unfortunately though, three got in.

He again, took off for the door. He saw Steele crouched down behind a Harley. He shouted his name and the VP's head snapped up. He pointed to the door and held up three fingers. Steele nodded, fired a shot at the Outlaw that was shooting at him, taking out his leg, then ran for the door too.

Both men practically barreled through the door in their haste to get inside. The door slammed violently against the wall. Then fire tore across Dragon's arm as a bullet hit him. He growled and turned towards the mother fucker that shot him. Then he watched as a bullet hit the

Outlaw square in the forehead. The man fell dead. He turned to Steele and nodded. Steele nodded back.

They headed back towards the bedrooms. Both men had their guns out and they moved in tandem. Dragon faced forward as they made their way down the hall and Steele was slightly behind him, angled so he could see behind them.

Suddenly, he heard Ali scream and then he heard two shots. Dragon swore and bolted down the hall. He stopped at the door to his room, seeing it lying on the floor, and cautiously stepped inside. There was a dead Outlaw laying in a pile of blood, half in and half out of the bathroom.

Turning to the bathroom, he found his Ali on the floor with an Outlaw on top of her. She was sobbing and thrashing, fighting to get him off. Dragon saw red. He roared and reached forward, grabbing the man by the back of his cut. He hauled him back and threw him into the wall of his room. Then he stomped towards the biker and punched him in the face over and over. When the man lost consciousness, Dragon didn't care and continued to pound on him. It took Steele pulling him away to get him to stop.

"We need to see what he knows," he ordered. "And dead men don't talk. Now see to your woman while I see if Trike's still alive."

Dragon immediately headed back into the bathroom. Ali

was still on the floor, her shirt was torn down the front and there were scratches on her chest. She was trying to crawl to Trike.

He reached her in two strides, leaned down and scooped her up, pulling her tiny body close to his. She screamed and hit him in the jaw. When she looked up and saw it was him, she cried out his name and threw her arms around his neck, holding on for dear life.

"You came for me," she cried.

"Always dewdrop," he said and sank to his knees.

Chapter Twenty-Four
Ali

Ali couldn't seem to get warm. Jaxon had cleaned the scratches on her chest, then taken off his own shirt and pulled it over her head. She had stopped shaking once the smell of him surrounded her. Then he had wrapped her in a blanket and pulled her in close.

Jax had kept her in their room ever since the shooting. A couple guys had come and removed the body and taken the unconscious biker out. Steele himself had taken Trike to see the doctor. Apparently, he was shot in the shoulder. He wouldn't be able to use his arm for a while, but he would heal, Jax had told her. Ali couldn't be happier about that. Trike held a special place in her heart ever since he had stapled the stars to Jax's ceiling.

Ali's scratches were the only injury she suffered. Her broken leg ached, but that was just from her moving it too much. Jax had been super protective since he found her. He refused to let anyone see her, and he refused to let her go. Ali was grateful for that. She wasn't ready to leave his arms yet. She snuggled closer and surprisingly fell asleep.

It wasn't long before she was woken by a knock on the door. Jax let her go and went over to open it. Preacher stepped into the room, looking directly at Ali.

"Need you to come and look at the bodies," he told her.

"No fucking way," Jax roared. He moved to stand in front of her and glared at his prez.

Preacher stepped aside so he could see them both. "Settle the fuck down brother," he ordered Jax. "I need her to make sure we got them all. The bodies are covered, I just need her to look at their faces. It will only take a minute. Old Joe took a look, but he wasn't there long, and didn't really know them. I wouldn't ask if there was another way."

"Okay," Ali told the men. Then she moved to get off the bed, leaning over to grab her crutches.

"Don't need those," Jax said, coming over and picking her up. Ali smiled at him. In the weeks she had been there, she had only used the crutches a couple of times. Every time she went to grab them, Jax would magically appear and cart her wherever she wanted. It was nice, but annoying at the same time.

Preacher led the way as Jax carried her through the common room and outside. The whole club was gathered around. There were about twelve bodies lying on the concrete with only their heads sticking out from under a large tarp. Jax approached them slowly, then set her on her feet at the end of the row. He kept his arms around her waist and she leaned back against him, giving him most of her weight.

The first three men she didn't recognize, but the fourth was one of the presidents three officers. She turned to Preacher and told him. He nodded and motioned for her to continue. The next two she had seen before, but didn't really know. She continued down the row pointing out one more officer.

She looked up to Jax. "The man you hit isn't here," she told him.

"No," Jax grunted. "We have him out back in the shed." Ali had heard about the shed, and she knew what happened to men that were kept there, so she left that one alone.

Preacher turned to her then. "Is this all of them?"

She looked to Jax, then over to Preacher. Quietly she told them, "the president's missing."

"Fuck me," Preacher muttered. "Dragon, take your girl around back for a bit and give her some peace. Brothers, let's take out the garbage."

Jax scooped her up again, and they headed away, towards the back of the compound. She loved it out back. There was a small lake at the far end of the property and it was surrounded by trees. Something else caught her eye though, something she couldn't remember ever seeing before. "Is that a cabin," asked Jax curiously.

Chapter Twenty-Five
Dragon

Dragon smiled at his Ali, then looked out towards the lake. She had seen the cabin. He moved on the bench of the picnic table and angled his body so he was facing hers.

"That cabin is mine," he told her. "About three months before you were taken I started building it. I know how much you love that lake, and with the surrounding woods, it makes it pretty private. I talked to Preacher about a year ago and asked if I could build there. He said I could. He wants to keep all the brothers close, so it works out for both of us. If anyone else finds their one, then they can build one too," he explained.

Ali had tears in her eyes, so he took her hand. "I love you Dewdrop. You're mine and will be until we're old and grey! But I don't want us living in a bedroom in the clubhouse. That's no place for my girl. It's pretty much done. The brothers have been helping while you were recovering. I haven't bought anything for inside it yet, I figured you could help with that."

Ali leaned over and placed her mouth against his, giving him a soft kiss. Dragon was having none of that. He dragged her across the picnic table so her body was pressed to his and threaded his fingers through her hair. Then he took over the kiss. He pressed his tongue against her lips and when she opened her mouth, he pushed inside. She touched her tongue to his, and he growled. Then he plundered, tangling their tongues together and stealing her breath. She went limp in his arms and he loved it.

When he slowed the kiss and then pulled away, he saw her eyes were still closed. He ran his nose down the side of hers and then kissed her forehead. She smiled and reached for his hand again. He figured that meant she liked the cabin.

"Can we move in," she asked him.

He signed. "As soon as this shit with The Outlaws is done, I promise we'll make the cabin our home. But it's safest for you at the clubhouse right now." She nodded her tiny head, and he knew that was her acceptance.

He loved that she never questioned him. It showed how much she trusted him. The dominant side of him liked that she gave him control. His Ali was the perfect fit for him.

Dagger came around the corner then and interrupted their time together. Dragon was actually surprised Preacher had given him as much time as he had.

"Brother," he said. "Preacher wants you inside. Get Ali back safely to your room and then he wants you to help question the Outlaw." Then he winked at Ali, turned away, and headed back inside.

"Come on Dewdrop, let's get you inside." Then he lifted her and headed into the clubhouse. She didn't say one word about what Dagger said as he took her back to his room.

Once inside, he settled her on the bed. When she was curled up in the fucking pink comforter with her book, he kissed her head and strode out of the room.

He met Dagger, Navaho, Steele and Preacher at the bar. They all did a shot of whiskey together, then made their way to the shed. As he opened the door and headed inside, he got a good look at the man hanging in cuffs from a chain in the ceiling.

The man glared at them as they lined up in front of them. His hair was longer and greasy. His clothes looked like they hadn't been washed in a week, and his vest was filthy. That was something his club wouldn't have tolerated. Your vest is an extension of your club. If your vest isn't in top shape, it's taken as a sign of disrespect.

He turned to the brothers with a smile on his face. "It's time to play," he said. "I'm gonna fire up the blowtorch."

The man's face turned a deathly shade of white and he started to beg. Now that's more like it Dragon thought.

Chapter Twenty-Six
Dragon

Dragon was furious. The biker in front of him had admitted to being the fucker that kept breaking his Ali's leg. It hadn't taken much, a few good punches from Navaho, and a few cuts with Steele's blade and the man was a blubbering mess.

They had questioned the biker about the presidents where abouts, but the man didn't know. Apparently, their prez had sent them in to retrieve his Ali and then they were to meet him down the road. He must have known it would be a blood bath, because he had sent his club to be slaughtered.

Dragon stood with the blowtorch ready. With no information of where the president was, there was no reason to keep the man alive. His Ali would never walk again without a significant limp, it was time for him to take his vengeance. His brothers surrounded the biker and Dragon stepped forward.

When Dragon got close, the man started screaming. He had no sympathy for him. When the blowtorch hit the man's leg and burned through his ratty jeans, the smell of burnt flesh hit the air. Dragon ignored the gagging noises coming from his brothers, and simply smiled in satisfaction.

"I god damned hate the smell when you do that," Dagger complained.

Dragon ignored him, pulling the torch away from the biker's leg. The biker was sobbing now and hanging limply from the chains. He put the torch to the man's other leg and did the same to it.

Dragon got close to the man's ear so he could whisper, "you hurt something that was mine. That girl owns mine heart and now I own yours," Dragon hissed furiously.

Then he lifted the blowtorch until it was level with the man's chest. Taking his time, and dragging it out, he positioned it over where the man's heart was. Then he slowly moved it forward and started to burn. The man thrashed, screaming and sobbing, but Dragon continued. Flesh melted away as the torch burned through it. The man soon stopped moving, and Dragon knew he was dead.

He stepped back and flicked off the torch, setting in

down in its holder to cool. He felt like a weight had been lifted. The president was still out there, but the rest of the club had been taken care of. It was a good day.

"Brother's," Preacher commanded. "A couple of prospects can clean this mess up. Dragon go shower, you smell like shit. We'll meet later and figure out where to go from here. It may end up being just a waiting game," he advised.

Steele spoke up. "Dragon, take my room and clean up there. No fucking way Tink can see you like that."

"Appreciated," Dragon told him. He took one last look at the body, smirked, and silently walked out.

Once in the shower, he ran the water as hot as he could and stepped under the spray. For the first few minutes he just let the water run over him. Blood ran down the drain. Melting flesh was messy.

Dragon scrubbed himself and washed his hair twice, then stepped out. He towelled himself off quickly then wrapped it around his waist. He swiped at the mirror with the back of his hand, and the steam cleared away. Making a split decision, he picked up Steele's razor and got to work.

Once done, he cleaned up and walked out wearing the towel. He dumped his clothes in a trash can on the way. His cut was safely folded and laying on the dresser. Nobody wore their cuts to the shed, the stains never came out.

When he opened the door and entered the room, his Ali looked up. She gasped and dropped her book. "You shaved," she said stunned.

"My Dewdrop missed my face," he told her. He moved close and sat on the side of the bed.

"Please don't cut your hair," she whispered. "I love it longer."

She raised both her hands and placed them on either side of his face. Then she stretched up to run her nose down his. He caught her lips in a soft, slow kiss. He felt her relax into him. He pulled his lips away from hers and looked down at the most precious thing in the world.

"Marry me," he ordered.

Chapter Twenty-Seven
Ali

Ali clung to Jax. "Yes, I'll marry you, oh my god yes," she cried. Tears streamed down her face. This was the happiest day of her life.

Jax reached behind her and opened the drawer of his night stand. Her pulled out a small box and flicked it open. Inside was a beautiful ring. The centre was a diamond solitaire, and it was surrounded by an infinity symbol made of more tiny diamonds. It took her breath away.

He took it out of the box. "I bought this a couple weeks before you were taken. I planned to take you down by the lake, when the cabin was finished, and propose. But, I can't wait anymore. I want everyone to know that you belong to me." He slid the ring on her finger.

She smiled up at him. "I love you Jax," she told him. Then she leaned forward and kissed him. He deepened the kiss, and she moaned. He pulled back slightly and grabbed the bottom of her shirt. Then he looked at her to make sure she was alright with this.

Ali smiled and raised her arms. The shirt was immediately gone, and she giggled at how fast he moved. He bent down and placed his warm lips just below her ear. She shivered when his breath tickled her neck. He licked a path down and across her shoulder, then gave a small nip. He moved back up and nibbled on her ear. It was heaven.

Then his hands moved behind her back and she felt the clasp of her bra release. She gave a little shake, and it fell off. He studied her hungrily for a minute, then leaned forward and took a nipple into his mouth. Her back arched as he sucked on it. Carefully, he lowered her to the bed as he switched to the other breast and gave it the same attention.

She ran her hands through his dark hair and grabbed on, pulling him back up for a kiss. He complied, and she thrilled at the taste of his tongue as it chased and caught hers. His hand wrapped possessively around her neck as he deepened the kiss.

After a minute, he released her mouth and moved down pulling her skirt with him. Then he carefully lifted her ass and pulled her underwear down, being extra careful with her casted leg. He stood for a minute and ripped his towel off and then he was back, covering her with his warm body. His muscled bulged as he held himself up, making sure not to give her too much of his weight.

She ran her hands up and down his arms, then moved them to his back. He always had a killer body, but the extra muscle he had put on thrilled her. She felt his thick cock rubbing back and forth across her entrance. Then he pushed slowly and was inside. He stilled once he hit her back wall and let her adjust to the size of him.

Ali waited a second, and when he still didn't move she wiggled a bit. He growled and took that as his cue, pulling out and gently pushing back inside. He moved so slowly back and forth it was torture. Ali ran her nails down his back in a silent plea to move faster.

He seemed to get the message as his hips started to pound against hers. She could feel her orgasm building and cried out his name as she fell over the edge. A few strokes later and he roared as he came too. Eventually, he slowed his strokes until he soon stopped all together.

He held her tight for a few minutes, then kissed the top of her head and carefully pulled out. She whimpered at the loss of him and watched as he moved towards the bathroom. She heard water running, then he was back.

She held still as he took a cloth he had warmed under the sink and gently washed the remains of their love making away. She smiled as he threw it in the direction of the bathroom.

He then laid down and gathered her close, pulling her tight against him. She placed her head on his shoulder and laid her hand against his heart. He grabbed the comforter and pulled it up, so they were covered.

"Sleep love," he whispered. Within seconds she drifted off, and as sleep took her, she dreamed only of him.

Chapter Twenty-Eight
Dragon

Another week had passed and there was no word on The Outlaws president. Dragon could tell his Ali was going stir crazy, but she was trying to hide it from him. She had gone through all the books he had left for her, and she had even flipped through his mechanics book on Harley-Davidson motorcycles. That one drove his brothers nuts. She literally followed them around for a week solid, asking them questions. It got to the point they would see her coming, and they'd run the other way. Dragon thought this was hilariously funny and told them it was payback for the pink comforter.

He also caught her sitting on the picnic table a couple times staring longingly at the cabin. A brother was always with her for protection, but it's like she didn't even know they were there. The brother would give him a quick call to let him know he was needed, and he'd come and scoop his Ali up, thinking up different things to distract her.

One day she was sitting in the common room staring at her cast. Dragon tried to engage her in conversation, but he just couldn't cheer her up. Suddenly, the door was thrown open and Steele strode in. He walked right up to Ali and picked her up. She gasped and held on to him. His brother then strode back out the door. Dragon followed, wondering what the fuck his brother was up to.

Steele stomped over to an old tractor and dropped Ali in the raised scoop. Dragon was livid, bellowing "what the fuck."

When he reached his Ali, he found she was cushioned by a ton of blankets. Then he had to jump out of the way when the tractor started up and headed right for him. Dagger was driving, and he would have killed the fucker, except his Ali was laughing. When he ran to catch up to the tractor, he caught sight of his Ali with a huge smile on her face. Dagger drove that tractor around the lot for hours while Ali hung out of the scoop. She talked about it for days.

Two days later, Trike came home from the hospital. They kept him longer than expected, but the prospect ended up with an infection. His Ali couldn't wait to see him, she had been pissed they wouldn't let her go to the hospital to visit. Trike would have to wear a sling for a week, but then he would pretty much be back to normal. He knew it killed Trike not to be able to ride his hog.

When Navaho walked in with Trike, all the brothers and Ali were gathered in the common room. Trike stopped just inside the door, unsure of why everyone was looking at him.

Then Preacher bellowed, "Trike, you mother fucker, get your god damned ass over here."

Trike looked absolutely terrified as he scanned the room, then walked to where Preacher stood.

"Take that fucking vest off," he ordered. Trike looked devastated as he slowly took off his sling and placed it on the table. Then he winced in pain and awkwardly shrugged out of his vest, handing it to the prez.

Steele came over and took the vest from Preacher, handing him a box at the same time. Preacher dropped the box on a table beside him and turned back towards an obviously saddened Trike.

When he cleared his throat Trike looked up at him. "Prospects have to be with the club a year before they even have a fucking chance of being patched in as a brother," Preacher explained. "Today we have an exception."

Trike's head instantly snapped up in confusion. Dragon knew the way Preacher was acting, the prospect figured they were cutting him loose.

"Due to Trike's fearless act in protecting a brother's woman and taking a bullet for her," he paused then. "And for thoughtfully putting the fucking stars on her ceiling, we've voted to fully patch you in as a member of this club. Congratulations brother," Preacher told him.

Then Preacher tossed the lid off the box and pulled out a new vest, with the official patch on the back. The brothers roared in approval and Trike wiped at his eyes as Preacher helped him pull it on.

Then Dragon's Ali left his side, to make her way slowly on her crutches to Trike. When she got to him, she was crying. She looked up at him. "I can't express how thankful I am for you protecting me that day. You got me in the bathroom and helped hold off the bikers until Jaxon could get to me. You took a bullet because of me, and for that I am truly sorry."

Then Dragon watched as Ali pulled Trike's head down and kissed his cheek. Trike smiled then and picked Ali up with his good arm, making her squeal and drop her crutches. Then he spun her in circles while she laughed.

Dragon saw red, and stormed in his direction, but the little fucker saw him coming. He set his Ali on her feet, then took off. Even with a messed up arm the fucker was fast.

"Fucking bikers," Dragon growled, and he heard Ali giggle.

Chapter Twenty-Nine
Ali

Ali was so excited about today as she was finally getting her leg cast off. This last week had been horrible. She just couldn't get comfortable, no matter how she positioned her leg, and the itchiness was driving her nuts. She had found a long, thin stick on the ground and had shoved it down the side of her cast, desperately trying to find some relief. Of course, when Jaxon found her doing this, he raised hell, and ripped the stick away from her. Then he broke it in half and lectured her on the dangers of scratching up her leg.

She rushed through her shower, really happy to have this be the last day she would have to Saran Wrap her leg. Dagger had put up a safety bar in the shower and installed a small bench at the end. It made it really easy to shower by herself even though she missed having Jaxon in the bathroom to help her. Jaxon wouldn't talk to Dagger for a week, insisting he did it on purpose just so he couldn't see her naked anymore. When Dagger called him a baby, a fifteen-minute wrestling match ensured.

Ali quickly towelled off and dried her long hair. Then she dressed in a t-shirt and another skirt. Her flip flops were the last thing to go on as she found them the easiest to get on. She only dabbed on a small amount of makeup before declaring herself ready.

When she exited the bathroom, she found Jaxon sitting on the bed. She couldn't stop the smile from appearing when she saw her big, bad biker sitting on the pink bed. He never once asked to get rid of it, just accepting that it was done to make her happy.

He scooped her up and gave her a long, deep kiss. She loved how affectionate he was towards her. Carrying her into the common room, he sat her at one of the tables. Navaho set down a plate in front of her. She salivated at sight of bacon, eggs, toast and cut up a melon, and gave him a big smile before digging in.

"You know," she told him, "I've gained back enough weight. You can calm down on the food now." He only grunted his disapproval and walked away. She smiled, knowing he wasn't going to change.

When she was done, Jaxon got her into a truck and some bikers mounted up to escort them to the hospital. She couldn't wait until she could get on the back of Jaxon's bike. They used to take long rides together all the time.

The hospital wasn't very busy, but it wouldn't have mattered anyway, as Doc rushed them into an empty room. She was surprised at how fast he cut the cast off, and then she got a look at her leg. It looked awful. It was so pale, it looked white, and the skin was flaking in some spots because it was so dry.

Doc explained that all she had to do was apply a cream to it in the morning and at night and it would help. He also told her to sit in the sun a bit to bring back some colour although he cautioned her to be careful as it would burn easily.

Then he whisked her up for a final X-ray. When the results proved everything was good, he showed her how to get her knee brace on and off. He explained her knee would still be a bit weak and the brace would help support it. She could also wear the brace over pants, which thrilled her.

The first steps were painful and Ali would have fallen if Jaxon wasn't there to catch her. She walked very slowly and her leg shook with each step. The limp was bad as the pressure caused her leg to collapse. Doc explained it would take a while to build up the strength in it again and suggested she get a cane for the first little while.

She wasn't happy, but she thanked him and Jaxon carried her out to his truck. She told him she needed to walk, but of course he wouldn't listen. Once she was settled, and they headed off, she turned to watch as the bikers revved their engines and followed. She just stared at them wistfully.

Chapter Thirty
Dragon

It was heart breaking to watch his Ali struggle. She had gotten her cast off three days ago and still had a hard time walking. The doctor assured her it was normal, but she was agonizing over it. Each step appeared painful for her, and a couple times her leg gave out and she fell. That was devastating to see. His Ali was so strong, but this was killing her. She kept trying and outright refused to let him carry her.

Then Navaho had surprised her with a cane. Apparently, he had carved it, and his mother had painted delicate pink butterflies up and down it. The cane was beautiful and Ali was overwhelmed, crying as she thanked him. At least this time she didn't give him a kiss, and the brother got to keep all his appendages!

The cane helped a lot, and his Ali didn't fall again. She

still struggled, and the limp was bad, but at least she didn't hurt herself any more. It was a balm to his already shot nerves.

To cheer her up, the brothers decided to have a BBQ and fire that night. It was to celebrate their engagement and Trike's patch in. Dragon thought it was a great idea and his Ali was thrilled.

He watched her get dressed in her skinny jeans and an off the shoulder cream sweater. She was beautiful. He helped her outside and sat her at one of the picnic tables. Dagger manned the BBQ and was cooking up a feast of chicken and ribs. Salads, buns and corn on the cob lined a fold-up table nearby.

Dragon filled two plates and brought them over to his Ali. When he sat down, she curled into his side and kissed his cheek in thanks. Instead of moving back over a bit, she stayed close to him and ate. He smiled, his Ali knew he wanted her close.

Steele and Preacher sat with them, and when Dagger finished grilling, he joined them as well. Ali was grilling them about when they were going to get their own girls, and Dragon laughed as he watched his brothers squirm. It was relaxing for both him and Ali, and he was grateful to his brothers for planning this.

When it started to get dark, they moved the party over to the fire pit and Navaho took over. It didn't take him long to get a huge fire blazing. The brothers sat on benches, and at picnic tables. When Ali tried to sit on a bench, Preacher stopped her. She looked unsure so Dragon stepped beside her and grabbed her tiny hand.

Laughter ensued, and they turned to see Dagger and Steele carting over a love seat that they had adorned with a massive pink bow.

"Fucking bikers," Dragon grumbled, but he sat when it was placed by the fire, pulling his Ali down beside him. She instantly melted into his side and he wrapped his arms around her.

Beers and liquor flowed as the men settled in to watch the flames. Old Joe even got out his guitar and played some old tunes, livening things up. Ali laughed as a drunk Trike tried to dance. When he got too close to the fire, a couple brothers declared him done and physically parked his ass in a chair.

When he caught his Ali starting to doze off. He picked her up and carried her to their room. He got her settled, then moved to join her. She instantly said no, telling him to go back out to the party. He tried to tell her it was fine, but she was insistent, so after a long, soft kiss he quietly left the room.

After finding a prospect to sit outside her door, he went back to his brothers. He settled in to enjoy a couple shots of whiskey and let off some steam.

Two hours later, a brother came out roaring that the

prospect was on the floor with his throat cut. They searched the clubhouse and woods, but his Ali was gone. You could hear Dragon's tormented wail for miles.

Chapter Thirty-One
Ali

Ali slowly woke knowing something wasn't right. It was a gut feeling, but she was learning to listen to them.
Quietly she eased to the side of the bed and slowly sat up. She had on loose pyjama pants and a lace tank top. She reached over and grabbed Jaxon's hoodie, slipping into it quickly. Taking her time, she stood, trying to keep pressure off her leg. She was halfway across the room when the door quietly opened.

"Jaxon," she called out tentatively.

"No princess," came the growled reply. She knew that voice, and the only man that called her that was the president of The Outlaws. She opened her mouth to scream, but he was immediately there, covering it with his huge hand. "I don't think so," he snarled at her.

He dragged her back to the bed and threw her down, making sure to keep his hand on her mouth. Then he reached behind him and pulled something out of his pocket. His hand left her mouth, and he shoved in a dirty rag. Then he grabbed another one and tied it around her head, securing the disgusting rag in her mouth. She tried to scream, but no sound came out.

Panicking, she thrashed and scratched, trying to get away from the biker. He raised his arm and punched her in the face. Pain immediately exploded in her cheek, and she felt blood, as it ran down her face. He must have sliced her with his ring. She cried out when he flipped her onto her stomach and painfully wrenched her wrists behind her. Luckily, she still had her bandanas on, so when he tied them together, the rope didn't touch her skin.

She tried to roll off the bed, back a painful knee to the back stopped her. He reached down and yanked her legs together, trying her ankles as well. When his knee was gone, she found she still couldn't move.

He flipped her over again, so she was on her back, then leaned in close. His breath smelled like stale cigarettes and alcohol, and she tried to turn away. He didn't seem to care, and she cringed when he leaned closer to whisper "mine," in her ear. She sobbed and shook her head no.

He laughed cruelly, then picked her up and threw her over his shoulder. It hurt, and she tried to wiggle away, but his grip was too strong. He quickly crossed the room, searched the hall a minute, then headed out the bedroom door. When he stepped over something she looked back, horrified to see a prospect she didn't know very well lying there. His throat was cut and his eyes stared up at her unseeing. She screamed, but the rag in her mouth muffled it.

He continued down the hall, then made his way through the common room. He exited the building with absolutely no one seeing him. She was terrified and could do nothing but cry as she watched the glow from the fire grow smaller and smaller. Nobody had any idea what was happening to her as not a sole had seen them.

He ignored the gate, as she was sure he knew someone was manning it, and followed the fence line for quite a while. Then he stopped and bent, and she was roughly thrown through a hole. She cried out when she hit the ground and watched as he got down and crawled through a cut in the fence after her. Immediately, he picked her up again, and she was once more back on his shoulder.

She figured he walked down the road for about ten minutes before he finally stopped. She heard something unlock and then lift. Then she was lowered into what she knew was a trunk. Panicking she tried to move, but couldn't, and watched in horror as he closed the lid, plunging her into darkness.

She heard him stomp to the front of the car and open a door. Then the car rocked as he got in and the door was slammed shut. She could do nothing but sob as he started the car and drove away. She wondered if she would ever get to see Jaxon again.

Chapter Thirty-Two
Dragon

Dragon was hurting, both physically and mentally. Three brothers had a hold of him. He had tore up the common room, smashing tables and chairs, and swearing bloody murder. He needed his Ali back, and he couldn't think straight without her. He had taken down anybody that had gotten near him, and the rage just kept building. His beautiful Ali had been taken. She survived once, but he didn't know if she could survive again. And he knew without a doubt, that if she died, he would too.

He pulled against the arms holding him. Finally, Preacher stepped in front of him. "Calm, brother," he roared in Dragon's face. "If you don't get a hold of yourself, I'm gonna lock you in the fucking shed, and you won't be a part of this. I know you're suffering, I know you feel helpless, and I know what that mother fucker did to your girl. You have the entire club behind you, you feel me brother," he growled.

Dragon bowed his head. "I feel you," he stated a bit more calmly. His prez was right, he was no help to anybody like this. The longer he raged, the longer his brothers had to wait to search for her. He shrugged out of their hold. "I'm calm," he forced out.

"Better be," Preacher stated. He turned to Navaho. "You find anything in his room that we can use?"

Navaho turned to look at Dragon. "Prospect is dead, no doubt about that. There's a bit of blood on the bed, but it's near the pillows. I'm thinking he hit her, maybe to knock her out, maybe just to subdue her. One trail leads out the door, so he had to be carrying her. I was going to follow it, see where it leads," Navaho explained.

Dragon clenched his fists, even a little of his Ali's blood was too much. She was suffering, and it killed him. He turned to Navaho, "lead the way brother."

Navaho headed outside, and he, Preacher, Steele and Dagger followed him. Trike looked on in longing, and Dragon nodded his head before heading out. Trike instantly moved to follow them. Navaho headed for the gate, then veered to the right, staring at the ground as he went.

When they came to the broken fence, Preacher swore. The huge bikers crouched down and pushed their way through. Navaho walked down the road silently for about ten minutes. Every one of them stayed close. No one said a word to distract the Indian, and no one questioned how Navaho tracked so well. His brother could see things no one else could.

He finally stopped and crouched down, searching the dirt and gravel. Silence reigned as they waited. After a few minutes, he stood.

Then Navaho explained. "A car was parked here, probably waiting. I don't think anyone was in it as it looked like the president got in the front seat. I see marks near where the back of the car would have been, so I'm assuming he put Tink in the trunk. Car went that way," and Navaho pointed to the right. "It's probably a later model sedan."

"How the fuck can you tell that," Trike questioned.

"Bigger tires, and the wheels are spaced further apart," Navaho told him. "But it doesn't ride as heavy as a truck or SUV."

"Damn," Trike said, as shook his head.

"Let's head back, grab our hogs, and head out," Preacher informed them. "And I want a fucking prospect here fixing this god damned fence," he roared.

The brothers all walked back down the road, at a brisk pace. They entered the clubhouse and took a minute to grab their pieces and head for their hogs. A couple more brothers followed, and they roared out the gates. Their bikes flew down the road. When they came to a split in the road, Navaho dropped his kickstand and took a look around. He pointed down one of the roads and they were off again.

It was nerve racking to stop every once in a while, so Navaho could do his thing. Dragon just wanted to go faster. His heart stopped beating the minute his Ali was taken, and he needed her back to start it up again.

Eventually, Navaho stopped and after looking down at the road for a while he turned to Dragon. His face was grim. Navaho had lost the trail.

Chapter Thirty-Three
Ali

Ali was utterly terrified. The trunk was dark, and it smelled like gas. She was light headed from the fumes. She could feel bruises forming on her poor body each time he turned a corner, and she was thrown around. With her hands and legs tied, there was no way to stop herself from banging against the sides. She had no idea where he was taking her, and that scared her to death.

She knew he wasn't taking her back to the cell. Jaxon had told her his club had been there, and they destroyed it. She felt the car slow down and turn again, and her head hit the side of the trunk. Her stomach rolled, but she wasn't sure if it was from the smell of the gas or the hit she just took.

Finally, the car slowed some more and came to a stop. She felt it rock, as the president got out, and heard his footsteps on the gravel as he walked away from her. She heard a door slam and then it was silent.

She squirmed and tried to loosen the ropes, but they were tied too tight and wouldn't budge. Tears fell down her cheeks as she realized she was helpless. There was no way to get free.

Ali thought of Jaxon then, her handsome biker. He meant everything to her, and she had just been returned to him. She had heard stories of how he had changed with her gone. She knew how the Dragon had come to be. She understood, and she loved both sides of him. She just wondered if he could handle losing her again.

She heard the door open and the president's footsteps, as he came to stand before the trunk. She pushed herself as far back as she could go as she heard the key turn in the lock. When the lid was thrown open, the bright light hurt her eyes.

He smiled at her and leaned in to grab her. She kicked her legs out and caught his arm. He howled as he pulled it back. She watched as his other arm came up, it was balled into a fist, and he slammed it into the side of her head.

She saw black spots as he roughly hauled her out of the truck. She was thrown over his shoulder again and the movement made her already pounding head hurt more. She welcomed the darkness this time when she finally passed out.

When she woke, she was lying on a cot in the middle of a run-down shack. It smelled musty inside, and she figured from the looks of things, it hadn't been lived in for a long time. There wasn't much light inside, as the windows were coated with dirt, but she could see the cabin itself was small. She swung her head to the left and found the president sitting in a chair watching her.

He eyed her as he stood slowly and made his way over to her. All she could see was the huge knife he had in his hand. He stopped when he was beside her and glared down at her. He moved the knife from hand to hand taunting her. She sobbed as she kept her eyes glued on the knife.

Suddenly, he reached down and grabbed her legs. With a quick flick of his wrist he sliced through the ropes binding them together. Her legs tingled as the circulation immediately started to come back in them. Her knee was throbbing, but she couldn't worry about that now.

He moved closer up the bed and grabbed her arm, rolling her to her side. Next, she found her hands were free as he sliced through those ropes as well. He rolled her to her back again as she tried to moved her arms. They hurt and wouldn't cooperate, hanging limply at her sides.

He moved up the bed again, this time grabbing a fistful of her hair and yanking her head off the bed. She whimpered as she felt the knife at the back of her scalp. He sliced through the rag and it fell free. Immediately, she spit out the one in her mouth, licking her dry lips. He let go of her hair and her head fell back on the bed.

When he moved to stand beside her again she screamed. He laughed as he climbed on the bed, sitting on her thighs with a smile on his face.

"I missed you," he told her. "Time to play," he growled as he leaned down towards her.

Chapter Thirty-Four
Dragon

Dragon was in agony, and he had no idea what to do. The longer they took to find his Ali, meant the longer she could be suffering. His window for getting her back in one piece was closing. He stared down each road in front of him, hoping for a sign, but there was nothing.

Preacher stomped to the front of the bikes and bellowed, "break up in two's. I want every road in this area searched. If someone's sitting on their front porch, question them. If you see any new tire tracks, follow them. If your gut tells you to check something out, you damn well check it the fuck out." Then he turned to Dragon and grabbed his shoulder. "Hold on brother, this isn't over yet."

Preacher turned to Navaho. "I want you with Dragon. Ride ahead a bit, you don't see a trail, you turn back and try the other way." He turned back to the brothers. "Mount up," he ordered and Harley's roared away in every direction.

Dragon spent the next two hours following Navaho. Preacher figured the Outlaw's president had to be close if he was watching the clubhouse. He knew exactly when to sneak in and take his Ali. That being said, they stuck to roads around the clubhouse. Dragon was worried that their theory was wrong.

The president could have stayed close by, but once he had Ali, why would he? He would know the bikers would come after him. If it was Dragon, he'd want to run with her. But, maybe the president didn't want to wait. If he was desperate to grab her, and had waited so long, maybe he would want to hurt her right away.

Dragon's head was spinning as he went back and forth with possibilities. All of them ended the same, Ali either hurt or dead. He couldn't get the picture of her broken body crouched down in the ditch out of his head. And, what if he hit her again, and her memory didn't come back this time?

Dragon shook his head to clear it of such thoughts. His Ali was strong, and she knew he would be looking for her, she'd hold on until he found her. When he did, he was holding on forever. Their wedding wouldn't be delayed, he would make sure she was bound to him for life.

Navaho was on the move again, so Dragon hit the throttle and the bike sped forward. They covered road after road, then turned around and started again. There were still no signs, and Dragon was scared.

Twenty minutes later Navaho's phone rang. Dragon pointed to the shoulder and Navaho nodded. When they were safely stopped, Navaho answered.

He grunted a couple times then stared at Dragon. When he hung up, he had Dragon's full attention. "Brother, talk to me," he pleaded.

"Dagger found an old man out cutting his grass. The old man saw a brown, late model sedan drive down the road about three hours ago. That fits our description and time frame. Roads a dead end, only thing at the end is a dilapidated hunting cabin. Hasn't been used in years. He also said the car never came back down the road, means it's still there," he told him.

He looked right into Dragon's hopeful eyes. "We've got him brother. We meet at the old man's house and go in on foot. It's only about a five-minute walk. You ready to end this fucker and get your woman back," he questioned.

"Hell yeah," Dragon replied relieved. It took seconds to get the bikes on the road, and then they were off. Dragon broke every speed limit and ignored the road signs, to get there as fast as he could. He didn't want to waste even a minute getting to his Ali.

When he pulled up at the old man's house, most of his brothers were waiting. He dropped his kickstand and joined them. The old man had informed them that the old hunting cabin was in off the road. This made things easier. They could walk straight down the middle of the road and they wouldn't be seen.

"Hold on Dewdrop, I'm coming," he promised.

Chapter Thirty-Five
Ali

Ali was pinned to the bed. The president had climbed on and was sitting on her thighs. Her knee was throbbing, but that was to be expected. She didn't have her brace on, and her knee got banged around pretty bad in the trunk. She was starting to get feeling back in her arms though, she just hoped it was enough.

He leaned down and put his hand around her neck. She thrashed and grabbed at it, desperately trying to pull it away. As soon as black spots started to appear behind her eyes, he let go. He did it twice more, and she was becoming weaker.

She tried to buck him off, but he was too heavy. He pulled at Jaxon's hoodie and forcefully ripped it from her body. She sobbed, fighting furiously now. Her nails dug into his arms, her fists hit his face, but he only laughed.

He reached back behind him and grabbed the knife. She had forgotten about it when he climbed on her and hadn't even known it was there. She froze as he raised it and cut the straps of her tank top. Then he put the handle in his mouth and grabbed the front of it, tearing it right down the middle.

She cried out and starting fighting harder. One of her fists hit him in the nose and blood tricked out, landing on her chest. She cringed and tried to move away, but he still retaliated by punching her back. The blow hit her in the side of her mouth and she tasted blood.

He lifted up and tore her pyjama pants off. She was completely naked now and terrified. With his head bent, he wasn't watching her, so she grabbed his hair and pulled as hard as she could. He was thrown off balance, so she bucked up. It was enough force that she actually knocked him off the bed.

She scrambled to her feet and started kicking him. He was down, but already moving to attack. He got on all fours and was trying to stand. She screamed and tried to get away. He grabbed her ankle before she could and yanked.

Ali hit the ground hard, but noticed the knife was near her hip. He saw it at the same time, and she struggled to try to reach it first. He grabbed her arm and wrenched it back, making her cry out. His free hand grabbed the knife.

With him pinning her arm to the floor she had no time to react, and he cut a line from her shoulder to just above her elbow. She screamed as a searing pain hit. Blood immediately starting running down her arm and he started at it, watching as it hit the floor.

She yanked her arm free and threw all her weight at him. He dropped the knife as he caught her, but his hands slipped in her blood. With nothing but escape on her mind, she grabbed the knife and plunged it into his side.

As he fell he bellowed, "you never fought this hard before, what the hell happened?"

"I didn't have anything to fight for before. You took my memories, but I have them now, and I have Jax. He's the other half of my soul, and he's coming for me," she yelled.

He sneered and started to rise, pulling the knife out as he grabbed the bed. She cried out and made a quick grab for Jax's hoodie. Once she had it, she stumbled to the door. Her knee wasn't holding her up very well, but she forced herself to keep going. She smashed through the door and fell down the steps. She could feel the scratches from the gravel on her side.

Ali heard him as he slowly made his way to the door. She scrambled up and ran for the trees. It was hard going, but she made it. She took a minute and struggled into the hoodie. Her arm was killing her, but she had to keep moving. She could hear him bellowing her name as he came after her.

She kept going, stumbling every once in a while, but keeping a distance between them. Jaxon, she thought, where are you. I need you.

Chapter Thirty-Six
Dragon

Dragon was practically running down the middle of the country road. He couldn't hold back, his Ali was so close he could feel her. No matter how many times Preacher yelled at him to slow down, he ignored him. Now he had all his brothers moving at a fast jog to keep up.

Finally, he saw the end of the road ahead. He could just make out the hunting cabin to the side. He picked up his pace and was soon in an outright sprint.

Suddenly, he was tackled from behind, and he hit the dirt at the side of the road. When he turned his head, Steele was climbing to his feet.

"Fucking hell," he growled at him. Brushing the dirt off as he got to his own feet.

Steele glared at him. "There are about fifteen bikers altogether. Do you know what fifteen bikers running down the fucking road wearing motorcycle boots sounds like?" Steele shook his head. "Use your head brother," he growled. Then he was off again, moving slowly closer to the cabin.

Dragon cursed, then followed, making sure he was quieter. He never had to be told what to do before, but this was his Ali, and he wasn't thinking rationally when it came to her. He was just desperate now.

When the bikers reached the cabin, they spanned out and moved forward cautiously. There appeared to be only the front entrance and a small window at the side. The cabin was deathly quiet, which made the men leery.

Dagger moved to the window and peered inside. His body stiffened, then he leaned in closer to get a better look. After signalling it was all clear, they moved to the door. Steele pushed it open, and they followed him inside.

Dragon came to an abrupt stop when he got a look around. The first thing he noticed was the blood. There was quite a bit of it on the floor beside a bed. He moved forward, his heart beating frantically. The blood was fresh as it was still a bright red. He seethed as he turned to the bed. You could tell it had been used, and that scared the hell out of him.

Navaho stepped forward and knelt down beside the

blood. He took a good look at the way it pooled on the floor, and then his eyes went for the door.

"Looks like they're both hurt," he stated. "Also looks like they both left the cabin." He got up then and went out the front door. All the brothers stayed right behind him. Navaho stopped at the bottom of the steps.

"Ali fell here," he said pointing to the indentation in the dirt. "Then she went into the trees. It looks like the president went after her." He then moved towards the trees. "I can follow the trail fairly easily from here." He turned back to Dragon. "Ali is lighter and barefoot, so her trail will be a bit harder, but the president is heavy and wearing boots, so it's his I'll follow."

Preacher nodded in agreement, and they were off. A couple brothers circled back and stayed at the cabin, just in case either Ali or the president headed back there.

Even Dragon could have followed the president, his trail was that obvious. His footprints were deep and branches were snapped off along the way. If that didn't do it, then you looked for the blood. Every couple steps they found blood, either on the path, or smeared on the trees. This meant they could move fairly quickly. Also, with the path being dirt, they didn't make much noise.

Dragon was getting anxious as they could tell they were close. I'm almost there Dewdrop, he thought. Then they heard footsteps up ahead and Ali's name being yelled.

Got you mother fucker, he thought. Collectively, his brothers snapped their heads in the direction of the yell, and they all tore through the woods. Fifteen bikers against one was pretty good odds.

Chapter Thirty-Seven
Ali

Ali was sobbing as she moved through the trees. She couldn't even count how many times she fell. She was pretty much dragging her bad leg now. Her arm had gone numb, but the sleeve of Jaxon's hoodie was wet with blood, making her shiver. Her face hurt too.

She found a thick branch on the ground and picked it up. Using it like a crutch helped, but she still moved slowly. Her head was making her dizzy, but she figured that could have been the blood loss.

She could hear the president stumbling through the woods, not too far behind her. She must have got him better than she thought because he stayed pretty even with her. Never gaining ground, but never falling behind either. It was his yelling though that put the fear in her heart. Every few minutes he would bellow her name.

She knew that if she could hear him moving behind her, he would be able to hear her. Neither one of them were being very quiet.

She pushed herself to keep moving. She was getting really tired now, but she knew she couldn't stop. She fell again and grabbed a tree to use it to haul herself back up. When she stood, her knee gave out again, and even with the branch, she couldn't hold herself up. She sobbed as she gave up and lay back on the ground.

She was shaking badly now, she was so scared and cold. She had to get back up, but she knew she couldn't. In desperation she started to drag herself along. Twigs and rocks scraped at her legs.

She saw a huge pine tree up ahead, its branches so low they touched the ground. She pulled her body towards it. Getting as far down as she could, she dragged herself under it, then curled up on her side to wait. There was nothing left in her, and she prayed he didn't find her.

She heard his footsteps getting closer and closer. Terrified, she covered her mouth, hoping he wouldn't hear her crying. She was sure he'd be able to hear her heart though, it was beating so fast. It even sounded loud to her ears.

He bellowed her name again as he moved closer. She whimpered and drew her legs up closer to her body. She could just make him out through the pine needles. He was searching around, and when he saw the tree, he smiled. He had found her.

She pushed up against the trunk and cried out. He dropped down beside the tree and laughed. Then all of a sudden, his hand shot under the branches and he grabbed her ankle. He started to pull, and she wrapped her arms around the trunk, trying desperately to hold tight. Her ankle hurt from the force of him pulling, but it was her good leg he had grabbed. She screamed as loud as she could as she kicked at him with her bad leg.

She finally kicked something solid, and he bellowed in pain letting go. She pulled her legs back in close to her body and tried to drag herself to the other side of the tree trunk. She saw his arm come back under the tree as he tried to reach for her again. He was cursing her now, but he couldn't quite get her.

Ali sobbed as she watched him wiggle his body along the ground, then he stuck his head under the tree. He smirked as he glared at her. She screamed as he reached out for her once more, this time getting a solid hold of her leg. As he wiggled his huge body back out from under the tree, he dragged her out with him.

She grabbed the tree trunk once more, desperately trying to stop him. He gave one huge yank, and she yelped as her arms were torn from around the tree. He dragged her completely out, then flipped her over. She looked up at his face and saw the rage in it.

She opened her mouth and screamed Jaxon's name as

loud as she could. He threw his head back and laughed "That fucking biker can't help you now," he sneered.

"Oh, yes he can," she heard roared from behind him.

Chapter Thirty-Eight
Dragon

Dragon tore through the woods and knocked some of his brothers out of his way. He was like a bear, charging to attack. The president yelled his Ali's name again, and Dragon ran in that direction. Then he heard a blood-curdling scream and his heart stopped. He picked up speed and charged to where the biker stood.

All his brothers came up behind him as he stopped just shy of the president. He had his back to them and didn't even realize they were there as he taunted his Ali. All he could see of her was her leg, the president was blocking the rest of her with his body.

When he roared at the president, letting him know he was there, the president startled slightly. Slowly, he turned around. When he saw all the bikers standing there, he turned a deathly white. The only weapon

Dragon could see on the man was a knife.

The president turned back to Ali, raising the knife and heading for her. At once, fifteen bikers drew their pieces and fired. The sound was deafening as all of them went off at the same time. Ali screamed.

The president dropped the knife, then sank to his knees. He gradually turned his head to face Dragon. Multiple bullets had torn through the biker's chest, making it a bloodied mess. The president blinked once, then fell to his side dead.

Finally, he got a look at his Ali. Her face was pretty banged up, and she had a decent cut on her cheek. Her legs were covered in scratches, and the bottoms of her feet looked raw. She was wearing his hoodie, and he was thankful she was so tiny. It fell almost to her knees and covered her completely. He didn't think she had anything on underneath as he had seen her torn pyjamas at the hunting cabin.

Tears streamed down his Ali's face as she looked up at him. "Jaxon," she whispered in desperation. He instantly moved and was kneeling beside her. She literally fell into his arms sobbing. He pulled her onto his lap and held tight.

When she cried out in pain, Dragon eased his hold and looked down at her. Through her tears she pointed to her arm. It was then he noticed his hoodie was wet, and it stuck to her skin. He gently set her on the ground and lowered the zipper on the front. Making sure to keep her covered, he pulled her arm out of the sleeve. She squeezed her eyes shut and bit her lip. He had to pull the hoodie away from the arm as it was stuck good.

When he saw the bloody mess, he cursed. Instantly, Steele and Dagger removed their cuts. They both grabbed the backs of their t-shirts and whipped them over their heads, handing them to him. The wound lay from her shoulder to her elbow and was bleeding badly.

Dragon took one of the t-shirts and wrapped her arm. When she cried out, he could feel her pain. The other t-shirt he tied in a knot around her arm to hold the first one in place. Carefully, he tucked her arm inside of the sweatshirt, but not in the sleeve. He figured that way she could cradle it against her chest.

Nobody spoke as Dragon picked up his Dewdrop as gently as he could and tucked her close to his body. Still crying, but not as bad now, she tucked her head into his neck and breathed deeply. His smell seemed to calm her more as he heard her sigh.

Trying not to jostle her too much, he headed back the way he came. It took them a good ten minutes to make their way back to the cabin. Once they cleared the trees Dragon noticed a truck had been brought close to the cabin.

He felt his Ali huff in agitation. When he looked down at her in question, she said, "when am I going to get to ride on the back of your bike?"

He stared at her in speechless silence for a second, then threw his head back and roared with laughter. He caught a couple of his brothers chuckling behind him.

His Ali was going to be just fine.

Chapter Thirty-Nine
Dragon

Dragon was thrilled with Ali's progress. It was a week later, and she was doing great. Her cheek had pretty much healed, and it had only left a small scar. The doc had dropped off some cream for it, that would make the scar almost disappear, if she used it for a while. He had taken out the stitches in her arm yesterday, and he told her she still needed to be careful, but it was just a precaution. She could use the cream on her arm too, but it would scar regardless.

Ali didn't care, because with all her scars, his brothers claimed her to be one of them now. His Dewdrop cried, and he growled at them all, knowing he couldn't take on the entire club. Her knee was still healing, but she was back on her feet and using her cane again.

Today finally, he was taking his Ali out on the Harley.

He had surprised her with her own vest this morning, declaring her his old lady. She loved it and had proudly put it on. Then she had ran at him and jumped into his arms. It took them an hour before they left the room after that as Ali declared she had to "thank" him.

He took her arm and helped her outside because she had left her cane back in their room. She looked cute in her pink t-shirt, tight jeans, cut and biker boots. Her long hair blew around her in the light breeze and he smiled down at her as she laughed. She was perfect, he thought.

He nudged her and pointed ahead, then watched as her mouth dropped open in stunned silence. Every brother in the club stood beside their Harley's ready to ride. She squealed beside him in excitement and he knew if she could have, she would have been jumping up and down.

He helped her towards his bike and strapped a helmet to her head. She pouted because nobody else wore one, but he wouldn't budge. Nothing would ever hurt his Ali again. He straddled his bike and reached back to support her as she climbed on. He turned the key and his bike roared to life. Seconds later everyone else powered theirs up too. The sound was defeating, but his Ali clung to him and kissed the back of his neck. She was thrilled.

They headed out and rode away from town. Dragon loved every minute of the ride, having his Ali pressed up against his back. She made sure to push her tiny hands under his shirt and the whole time he felt her warmth against his stomach. They road for two hours along the winding back roads.

When they finally stopped, he dismounted and stepped in front of his Ali. She looked at the building they had parked in front of, then up at him curiously. He ignored her and leaned over to unstrap her helmet. He stowed it in his saddlebag and pulled out a brush. He did a spinning motion with his finger and she obediently turned around. Carefully, he brushed her hair, then replaced the brush in the saddlebag.

In one quick move, he put his hands on her waist and lifted her off the bike. Then he took her arm and helped her walk into the building. He loved her reaction as she realized where she was. All his brothers had filed in while he was looking after her and now sat in the benches in the court house. A court official stood at the front waiting to marry them.

Tears streamed down her face as she looked up at him. "Are you ready to officially become mine", he asked her. She nodded, as she clung to his arm. "Good," he stated, "because I need my ring on your finger."

Trike ran up then and placed a veil on her head and handed her a fresh bouquet of pink flowers. Then he stood to the side, with a smile and a camera in his hands. "Fucking bikers," Dragon laughed.

He walked her down the aisle. They answered when the officiant prompted them to, and then they were declared husband and wife. Dragon didn't wait to be told he could kiss her, he picked her up, spun her in circles and kissed her for all he was worth.

When he set her down, she was beaming and blushing, and his brothers were whooping. He couldn't be happier.

Epilogue

That very night Jaxon moved them into the cabin. It was beautiful. The front of it was filled with huge floor to ceiling windows that showcased the lake. Ali couldn't wait to sit in front of it and watch the sun set. It was an open floor plan, with the living room facing the lake, and a small kitchen off to the side. It had three bedrooms and two baths. The master had its own bathroom, and the two other bedrooms shared a bathroom. It also had a wrap-around porch and stairs that led down to the water. It was absolutely perfect.

It wasn't furnished except for a bed, as Jaxon promised the next day he would take her out to pick up furniture. He wanted her to pick out things she liked. The living room had a huge fireplace, and Ali was delighted at what he had done. A soft rug had been placed in front of it, and a fire had been lit. A picnic style meal had been laid out and a bottle of wine was chilling in a bucket.

A tear ran down her cheek as she looked up at her husband and whispered, "I love you".

He said it back passionately, then he kissed her. Pulling away slightly, he helped her over to the fireplace and then picked her up and placed her on the rug. She loved how he still made excuses to pick her up all the time.

Jaxon pulled the wine out of the bucket and poured two glasses. When he handed her one, she shook her head, taking both glasses out of his hands and placing them on the floor. She looked up at him and smiled.

"You seem to be full of surprises today," she mentioned, then she smiled at him shyly.

"Well I think I need to share one of my own." She paused for a minute before continuing. "When you found me the first time, I had to take a prescription, so my leg wouldn't get infected." She glanced down at her leg, then slowly raised her head again to look at him.

"I'm pregnant," she whispered happily.

Jaxon seemed frozen for a minute, then he let out a loud roar. "I'm gonna be a dad," he stated enthusiastically.

"You're gonna be a dad," she agreed.

He moved the picnic to the floor beside her and pushed her down. Then he slowly climbed over her and proceeded to make love to her all night long. She got to see the sun set that night, and the night after that, and the night after that...

About the Author

MEGAN FALL is a mother of three who helps her husband run his construction business. She has been writing all her life, but with a push from her daughter, started publishing. It's the best thing she ever did. When she's not writing, you can find her at the beach. She loves searching for rocks, sea glass, driftwood and fossils. She believes in ghosts, collects ridiculous amounts of plants, and rides on the back of her hubby's motorcycle.

MEGAN FALL

Look for these books coming soon!

STONE KNIGHTS MC SERIES
Finding Ali (Published)
Saving Cassie
Loving Misty
Rescuing Tiffany
Guarding Alexandria
Protecting Fable
Surviving November
Sheltering Macy
Defending Zoe

DEVILS SOLDIERS MC SERIES
Resisting Diesel
Surviving Hawk

THE ENFORCER SERIES
The Enforcer
The Enforcers Revenge

Finding Cassie
Stone Knight's Book 2

Chapter One
Cassie

Cassie cried out as she collapsed to the floor. The blow was hard, but she knew it wasn't hard enough to draw blood. Parker knew how much strength to use when he hit her, so it wouldn't leave a mark. Heaven forbid he left a bruise that she couldn't cover up. If he marked her face, he always made sure she iced the are thoroughly, to prevent it from swelling.

She remained on the ground so she didn't provoke him further and kept her eyes on the floor. Tonight he was in a good mood, so he huffed and lumbered away. She remained where she was and waited until she heard the bedroom door slam. Seconds later it came, and she breathed a sigh of relief.

She pushed herself up carefully and made her way to the kitchen. She opened the freezer and pulled out her trusty bag of peas. She knew it was a night she required them. After a year of abuse, she could just tell.

She made her way back to the couch and plopped down. Gently, she lifted the peas and settled them on her cheek. She flinched at the cold, but then moaned in relief as the pain gradually subsided. Tomorrow would be a good day, the swelling would be minimal and the bruising would be light enough to cover with a bit of makeup. She sighed, recognizing she got off lucky tonight.

She thought back to when she first met Parker. Her parents were incredibly strict and raised her with practically no freedom. She had to dress a particular way, she had to act a certain way, and she could only be friends with a certain type of people.

Her life had been hard growing up. Her father was a partner in a huge law firm and never had time for her. Her mother was a socialite, and there were a dozen charities and functions she needed to attend. Her parents were never home, and Cassie relished the time alone. She could breathe when they weren't around, and she didn't have to fret about being the perfect daughter.

She went on lots of dates, her parents made sure of that. Unfortunately, she despised all the boys, then later men, her parents insisted on setting her up with. They were boring stuck up rich kids, who were merely out to suck up to her father. They knew a marriage to her was a full ride in his prestigious law firm. They didn't care about her, they cared about the prestige she would bring and the money they would earn.

That's how she met Parker. Her parents pressured her to go on yet another date. If she wished to stay in their house, she had to adhere to their rules. She had gotten ready for the date the same way she had for all the others, but when the doorbell rang and she got a look at him, her heart fluttered. He was taller than most of the men her parents set her up with. He had short blonde hair and the most beautiful blue eyes. He wasn't dressed in a suit, like the rest usually were.

Instead, he wore jeans and a button up dress shirt. When he smiled at her, she couldn't help but smile back.

He showed her the attention and love she had been craving from her parents. They dated for two years before he proposed. At twenty two, she thought she loved him. He took her for romantic dinners, he bought her extravagant gifts and he seemed to put her before her parents.

He was a dream come true, and she was smitten. Unfortunately, once they were married, he showed his true colours. On their wedding night, he sat her down and explained how it was going to be. She was to act to the part of the adoring wife and he would be discreet about the other women he was sleeping with. She was to remain home, cooking the meals and managing the house, while he went out drinking with the boys and sleeping with whoever caught his attention that week.

Her life turned upside down in a minute, and not for the better. She learned her place quickly, because if she didn't, there would be repercussions. Tonight was just a small one, all because she inquired how his day went.